HIGH STAKES . . .

"Whips along as smoothly and as quickly as a thoroughbred running free"
—*San Francisco Examiner*

"As full of sudden and unexpected hazards as a first-class steeplechase" —*Heywood Hale Broun*

"One of Mr. Francis' most admirable and satisfying entertainments" —*The New Yorker*

"Fun, exciting, and vintage Francis"
—*Boston Globe*

"ONE OF HIS BEST!" —*Minneapolis Tribune*

Books by Dick Francis

Blood Sport
Bonecrack
Dead Cert
Enquiry
Flying Finish
For Kicks
Forfeit
High Stakes
In the Frame
Knockdown
Nerve
Odds Against
Rat Race
Risk
Slayride
Smokescreen
Trial Run
Whip Hand

Published by POCKET BOOKS

DICK FRANCIS
High Stakes

PUBLISHED BY POCKET BOOKS NEW YORK

POCKET BOOKS, a division of Simon & Schuster, Inc.
1230 Avenue of the Americas, New York, N.Y. 10020

Published by arrangement with Harper & Row, Publishers, Inc.
Library of Congress Catalog Card Number: 75-25082

ISBN: 0-671-46423-X

First Pocket Books printing July, 1977

10 9 8 7

POCKET and colophon are registered trademarks
of Simon & Schuster, Inc.

Printed in the U.S.A.

1

I looked at my friend and saw a man who had robbed me. Deeply disturbing. The ultimate in rejection.

Jody Leeds looked back at me, half smiling, still disbelieving.

"You're *what?*"

"Taking my horses away," I said.

"But . . . I'm your *trainer*." He sounded bewildered. Owners, his voice and expression protested, never deserted their trainers. It simply wasn't done. Only the eccentric or the ruthless shifted their horses from stable to stable, and I had shown no signs of being either.

We stood outside the weighing room of Sandown Park racecourse on a cold windy day, with people scurrying past us carrying out saddles and number cloths for the next steeplechase. Jody hunched his shoulders inside his sheepskin coat and shook his bare head. The wind blew his straight brown hair across his eyes and he pulled it impatiently away.

"Come on, Steven," he said. "You're kidding me."

"No."

Jody was short, stocky, twenty-eight, hard-working, clever, competent, and popular. He had been my constant adviser since I had bought my first race horses three years earlier, and right from the beginning he had robbed me round the clock and smiled while doing it.

"You're crazy," he said. "I've just won you a race."

We stood, indeed, on the patch of turf where winners were unsaddled: where Energise, my newest and glossiest hurdler, had recently decanted his smiling jockey, had stamped and steamed and tossed his head with pride, and accepted the crowd's applause as simply his due.

The race he had won had not been important, but the way he had won it had been in the star-making class. The sight of him sprinting up the hill to the winning post, a dark streak of rhythm, had given me a rare bursting feeling of admiration, of joy—probably even of love. Energise was beautiful and courageous and chock-full of will to win, and it was because he had won, and won in that fashion, that my hovering intention to break with Jody had hardened into action.

I should, I suppose, have chosen a better time and place.

"I picked out Energise for you at the sales," he said.

"I know."

"And all your other winners."

"Yes."

"And I moved into bigger stables because of you."

I nodded briefly.

"Well . . . you can't let me down now."

Disbelief had given way to anger. His bright-blue eyes sharpened to belligerence and the muscles tightened round his mouth.

"I'm taking the horses away," I repeated. "And we'll start with Energise. You can leave him here when you go home."

"You're mad."

"No."

"Where's he going, then?"

Actually, I had no idea. I said, "I'll make all the arrangements. Just leave him in the stable here, and go home without him."

"You've no right to do this." Full-scale anger blazed in his eyes. "You're a bloody rotten *shit.*"

But I had every right. He knew it and I knew it. Every owner had the right at any time to withdraw his custom if he was dissatisfied with his trainer. The fact that the right was seldom exercised was beside the point.

Jody was rigid with fury. "I am taking that horse home with me, and nothing is going to stop me."

His very intensity stoked up in me an answering determination that he should not. I shook my head decisively. I said, "No, Jody. The horse stays here."

"Over my dead body."

His body, alive, quivered with pugnaciousness.

"As of this moment," I said, "I'm canceling your authority to act on my behalf, and I'm going straight into the weighing room to make that clear to all the authorities who need to know."

He glared. "You owe me money," he said. "You can't take your horses away until you've paid."

I paid my bills with him on the nail every month, and owed him only for the current few weeks. I pulled my checkbook out of my pocket and unclipped my pen.

"I'll give you a check right now."

"No, you bloody well won't."

He snatched the whole checkbook out of my hand and ripped it in two. Then, he threw the pieces over his shoulder, and all the loose halves of the checks scattered in the wind. Faces turned our way in astonishment, and the eyes of the press came sharply to life. I couldn't have chosen anywhere more public for what was developing into a first-class row.

Jody looked around him. Looked at the men with notebooks. Saw his allies.

His anger grew mean.

"You'll be sorry," he said. "I'll chew you into little bits."

The face that five minutes earlier had smiled with cheerful decisive friendliness had gone for good. Even if I now retracted and apologized, the old relationship could not be re-established. Confidence, like Humpty Dumpty, couldn't be put together again.

His fierce opposition had driven me further than I had originally meant to go. All the same, I still had the same objective, even if I had to fight harder to achieve it.

"Whatever you do," I said, "you won't keep my horses."

"You're ruining me!" Jody shouted.

The press advanced a step or two.

Jody noticed. Maliciousness flooded through him and twisted his features with spite. "You big rich bastards don't give a damn who you hurt."

I turned abruptly away from him and went into the weighing room, and there carried out my promise to disown him officially as my trainer. I signed forms canceling his authority to act for me, and for good measure also included a separate handwritten note to say that I had expressly forbidden him to remove Energise from Sandown Park. No one denied I had the right; there was just an element of coolness toward an owner who was so vehemently and precipitously ridding himself of the services of the man who had ten minutes ago given him a winner.

I didn't tell them that it had taken a very long time for the mug to face the fact that he was being conned. I didn't tell them how I had thrust the first suspicions away as disloyalty and had made every possible allowance before being reluctantly convinced.

I didn't tell them, either, that the reason for my determination now lay squarely in Jody's first reaction to my saying I was removing my horses.

Because he hadn't, not then or afterward, asked the one natural question.

He hadn't asked *why*.

When I left the weighing room, both Jody and the press had gone from the unsaddling enclosure. Racegoers were hurrying toward the stands to watch the imminent steeplechase, the richest event of the afternoon, and even the officials with whom I'd just been dealing were dashing off with the same intent.

I had no appetite for the race. Decided, instead, to go down to the racecourse stables and ask the gatekeeper there to make sure Energise didn't vanish in a puff of smoke. But as the gatekeeper was there to prevent villainous strangers walking *in,* and not any bona-fide race horses walking *out,* I wasn't sure how much use he would be even if he agreed to help.

He was sitting in his sentry box, a middle-aged sturdy figure in a navy-blue serge uniform with brass buttons. Various lists on clipboards hung on hooks on the walls, alongside an electric heater fighting a losing battle against the December chill.

"Excuse me," I said. "I want to ask you about my horse—"

"Can't come in here," he interrupted bossily. "No owners allowed in without trainers."

"I know that," I said. "I just want to make sure my horse stays here—"

"What horse is that?"

He was adept at interrupting, like many people in small positions of power. He blew on his fingers and looked at me over them without politeness.

"Energise," I said.

He screwed up his mouth annd considered whether to answer. I supposed that he could find no reason against it except natural unhelpfulness, because in the end he said grudgingly, "Would it be a black horse trained be Leeds?"

"It would."

"Gone, then," he said.

"Gone?"

" 'Sright. Lad took him off, couple of minutes ago." He jerked his head in the general direction of the path down to the area where the motor horse boxes were parked. "Leeds was with him. Ask me, they'll've driven off by now." The idea seemed to cheer him. He smiled.

I left him to his sour satisfaction and took the path at a run. It led down between bushes and opened abruptly straight onto the graveled acre where dozens of horse boxes stood in haphazard rows.

Jody's box was fawn with scarlet panels along the sides; and it was already maneuvering out of its slot and turning to go between two of the rows on its way to the gate.

I slid my binoculars to the ground and left them, and fairly sprinted. Ran in front of the first row of boxes, and raced round the end to find Jody's box completing a turn about thirty yards away, and accelerating straight toward me.

I stood in its path and waved my arms for the driver to stop.

The driver knew me well enough. His name was Andy-Fred. He drove my horses regularly. I saw his face, looking horrified and strained, as he put his hand on the horn button and punched it urgently.

I ignored it, sure that he would stop. He was advancing between a high wooden fence on one side and the flanks of parked horse boxes on the other, and it wasn't until there was no sign he knew what his brakes were for that it occurred to me that maybe Energise was about to leave over *my* dead body, not Jody's.

Anger, not fear, kept me rooted to the spot.

Andy-Fred's nerve broke first, thank God, but only just. He wrenched the wheel round savagely when the massive radiator grill was a bare six feet from my annihilation and the diesel throb was a roar in my ears.

He had left it too late for braking. The sudden swerve took him flatly into the side of the foremost of the parked boxes, and with screeching and tearing sounds of metal the front corner of Jody's box plowed forward and inward until the colliding doors of the cabs of both vehicles were locked in one crumpled mess. Glass smashed and tinkled and flew about with razor edges. The engine stalled and died.

The sharp bits on the front of Jody's box had missed

me, but the smooth fender caught me solidly as I leaped belatedly to get out of the way. I lay where I'd bounced, half against the wooden fence, and wholly winded.

Andy-Fred jumped down unhurt from the unsmashed side of his cab and advanced with a mixture of fear, fury, and relief.

"What the bloody hell d'you think you're playing at?" he yelled.

"Why . . . didn't. . . . you . . . stop?" I said weakly.

I doubt if he heard me. In any case, he didn't answer. He turned instead to the exploding figure of Jody, who arrived at a run along the front of the boxes, the same way that I had come.

He practically danced with rage when he saw the crushed cabs.

"You stupid *bugger!*" he shouted at Andy-Fred. "You stupid sodding effing—"

The burly box driver shouted straight back, "He stood right in my way!"

"I told you not to stop."

"I'd've killed him."

"No, you wouldn't."

"I'm telling you. He stood there. Just stood there."

"He'd've jumped if you'd kept on going. You stupid bugger. Just look what you've done. You stupid . . ."

Their voices rose, loud and acrimonious, into the wind. Further away the commentator's voice boomed over the public address system, broadcasting the progress of the steeplechase. On the other side of the high wooden fence, the traffic pounded up and down the London-to-Guildford road. I gingerly picked myself off the cold ground and leaned against the weathered planks.

Nothing broken. Breath coming back. Total damage: all the buttons missing from my overcoat. There was a row of small right-angled tears down the front where the buttons had been. I looked at them vaguely and knew I'd been lucky.

Andy-Fred was telling Jody at the top of his raucous

voice that he wasn't killing anyone for Jody's sake, he was bloody well not.

"You're fired!" Jody yelled.

"Right!"

He took a step back, looked intensely at the mangled horse boxes, looked at me, and looked at Jody. He thrust his face close to Jody's and yelled at him again, *"Right!"*

Then he stalked away in the direction of the stables and didn't bother to look back.

Jody's attention and fury veered sharply toward me. He took three or four purposeful steps and yelled, "I'll sue you for this!"

I said, "Why don't you find out if the horse is all right?"

He couldn't hear me for all the day's other noises.

"What?"

"Energise," I said loudly. "Is he all right?"

He gave me a sick hot look of loathing and scudded away round the side of the box. I followed more slowly. Jody yanked open the groom's single door and hauled himself up inside, and I went up after him.

Energise was standing in his stall quivering from head to foot and staring wildly about with a lot of white round his eyes. Jody had packed him off still sweating from his race, and in no state anyway to travel, and the crash had clearly terrified him; but he was nonetheless on his feet, and Jody's anxious search could find no obvious injury.

"No thanks to you," Jody said bitterly.

"Nor to you."

We faced each other in the confined space, a quiet oasis out of the wind.

"You've been stealing from me," I said. "I didn't want to believe it. But from now on I'm not giving you the chance."

"You won't be able to prove a thing."

"Maybe not. Maybe I won't even try. Maybe I'll write off what I've lost as the cost of my rotten judgment in liking and trusting you."

He said indignantly, "I've done bloody well for you."

"And out of me."

"What do you expect? Trainers aren't in it for love, you know."

"Trainers don't all do what you've done."

A sudden speculative look came distinctly into his eyes. "What have I don't then?" he demanded.

"You tell me," I said. "You haven't even pretended to deny you've been cheating me."

"Look, Steven, you're so bloody unworldly. All right, so maybe I have added a bit on here and there. If you're talking about the time I charged you traveling expenses for Hermes to Haydock the day they abandoned for fog before the first—well, I know I didn't actually *send* the horse. He went lame that morning and couldn't go. But trainer's perks. Fair's fair. And you could afford it. You'd never miss thirty measly quid."

"What else?" I said.

He seemed reassured. Confidence and a faint note of defensive wheedling seeped into his manner and voice.

"Well . . ." he said. "If you ever disagreed with the totals of your bills, why didn't you query it with me? I'd've straightened things out at once. There was no need to bottle it all up and blow your top without warning."

Ouch, I thought. I hadn't even checked that all the separate items on the monthly bills did add up to the totals I'd paid. Even when I was sure he was robbing me, I hadn't suspected it would be in any way so ridiculously simple.

"What else?" I said.

He looked away for a second, then decided that I couldn't, after all, know a great deal.

"Oh, all right," he said, as if making a magnanimous concession. "It's Raymond, isn't it?"

"Among other things."

Jody nodded ruefully. "I guess I did pile it on a bit,

charging you for him twice a week when some weeks he only came once."

"And some weeks not at all."

"Oh, well," said Jody deprecatingly. "I suppose so, once or twice."

Raymond Child rode all my jumpers in races and drove fifty miles some mornings to school them over fences on Jody's gallops. Jody gave him a fee and expenses for the service, and added them to my account. The twice-a-week schooling-session fees had turned up regularly for the whole of July, when in fact, as I had very recently and casually discovered, no horses had been schooled at all and Raymond himself had been holidaying in Spain.

"A tenner here or there," Jody said persuasively. "It's nothing to you."

"A tenner plus expenses twice a week for July came to over a hundred quid."

"Oh." He tried a twisted smile. "So you really have been checking up."

"What did you expect?"

"You're so easygoing. . . . You've always paid up without question."

"Not any more."

"No. Look, Steven, I'm sorry about all this. If I give you my word there'll be no more fiddling on your account . . . If I promise every item will be strictly accurate . . . Why don't we go on as before? I've won a lot of races for you, after all."

He looked earnest, sincere, and repentant. Also totally confident that I would give him a second chance. A quick canter from confession to penitence, and a promise to reform, and all could proceed as before.

"It's too late," I said.

He was not discouraged; just piled on a bit more of the ingratiating manner that announced, "I know I've been a bad bad boy, but now I've been found out I'll be angelic."

"I suppose having so much extra expense made me behave stupidly," he said. "The mortgage repayments on the new stables are absolutely bloody, and as you know I only moved there because I needed more room for all your horses."

My fault now that he had had to steal.

I said, "I offered to build more boxes at the old place—"

"Wouldn't have done," he interrupted hastily; but the truth of it was that the old place had been on a plain and modest scale where the new one was frankly opulent. At the time of the move, I had vaguely wondered how he could afford it. Now, all too well, I knew.

"So let's call this just a warning, eh?" Jody said cajolingly. "I don't want to lose your horses, Steven. I'll say so frankly. I don't want to lose them. We've been good friends all this time, haven't we? If you'd just *said* . . . I mean, if you'd just said, 'Jody, you bugger, you've been careless about a bill or two—' well, I mean, we could have straightened it out in no time. But—well, when you blew off without warning, just said you were taking the horses away, straight after Energise won like that—well, I lost my temper real and proper. I'll admit I did. Said things I didn't mean. Like one does. Like everyone does, when they lose their temper."

He was smiling in a counterfeit of the old way, as if nothing at all had happened. As if Energise were not standing beside us sweating in a crashed horse box. As if my overcoat were not torn and muddy from a too close brush with death.

"Steven, you know me," he said. "Got a temper like a bloody rocket."

When I didn't answer at once, he took my silence as acceptance of his explanations and apologies, and briskly turned to practical matters.

"Well, now, we'll have to get this lad out of here." He slapped Energise on the rump. "And we can't get the ramp down until we get this box moved away from that other one." He made a sucking sound through his teeth. "Look, I'll try to back straight out again. Don't see why it shouldn't work."

He jumped out the back door and went round to the front of the cab. Looking forward through the stalls, I could see him climb into the driver's seat, check the gear lever, and press the starter: an intent, active, capable figure dealing with an awkward situation.

The diesel started whirred and the engine roared to life. Jody settled himself, found reverse gear, and carefully let out the clutch. The horse box shuddered and stood still. Jody put his foot down on the accelerator.

Through the windshield I could see two or three men approaching, faces a mixture of surprise and anger. One of them began running and waving his arms about in the classic reaction of the chap who comes back to his parked car to find it dented.

Jody ignored him. The horse box rocked, the crushed side of the cab screeched against its mangled neighbor, and Energise began to panic.

"Jody, stop!" I yelled.

He took no notice. He raced the engine harder, took his foot off the accelerator, then jammed it on again. Off, on, repeatedly.

Inside the box, it sounded as if the whole vehicle were being ripped in two. Energise began whinnying and straining backward on his tethering rope and stamping about with sharp hoofs. I didn't know how to begin to soothe him, and could hardly get close enough for a pat, even if that would have made the slightest difference. My relationship with horses was along the lines of admiring them from a distance and giving them carrots while they were safely tied up. No one had briefed me about dealing with a hysterical animal at close quarters in a bucketing biscuit tin.

With a final horrendous crunch, the two entwined cabs tore apart and Jody's box, released from friction, shot backward. Energise slithered and went down for a moment on his hindquarters and I, too, wound up on the floor. Jody slammed on the brakes, jumped out of the cab, and was promptly clutched by the three new-comers, one now in a full state of apoplectic rage.

I stood up and picked bits of hay off my clothes and regarded my steaming, foam-flaked, terrified four-footed property.

"All over, old fellow," I said.

It sounded ridiculous. I smiled, cleared my throat, tried again. "You can cool off, old lad. The worst is over."

Energise showed no immediate signs of getting the message. I told him he was a great horse, he'd won a great race, he'd be king of the castle in no time, and that I admired him very much. I told him he would soon be rugged up nice and quiet in a stable some-where, (though I hadn't actually yet worked out exact-ly which one) and that doubtless someone would give him some excessively expensive hay and a bucket of nice cheap water and I dared say some oats and stuff like that. I told him I was sorry I hadn't a carrot in my pocket at that moment but I'd bring him one next time I saw him.

After a time, this drivel seemed to calm him. I put out a hand and gave his neck a small pat. His skin was wet and fiery hot. He shook his head fiercely and blew out vigorously through black moist nostrils, but the staring white no longer showed round his eye, and he had stopped trembling. I began to grow interested in him in a way that had not before occurred to me: as a personality who happened also to be a horse.

I realized I had never before been alone with a horse. Extraordinary, really, when Energise was the twelfth I'd owned. But race-horse owners mostly patted their horses in stables with lads and trainers in atten-dance, and in parade rings with all the world looking on, and in unsaddling enclosures with friends pressing round to congratulate. Owners who, like me, were not riders themselves and had nowhere of their own to turn horses out to grass seldom ever spent more than five consecutive minutes in a horse's company.

I'd spent longer with Energise in that box than in all the past five months since I'd bought him.

Outside, Jody was having troubles. One of the men had fetched a policeman, who was writing purposefully in a notebook. I wondered with amusement just how Jody would lay the blame on my carelessness in walking in front of the box and giving the driver no choice but to swerve. If he thought he was keeping my horses, he would play it down. If he thought he was losing them, he'd be vitriolic. Smiling to myself, I talked it over with Energise.

"I don't know why," I said, "I haven't told him yet that I know about his other fraud, but as it turns out I'm damn glad I haven't."

"Do you know?" I said. "All those little fiddles he confessed to, they're just froth."

Energise was calm enough to start drooping with tiredness. I watched him sympathetically.

"It isn't just a few hundred quid he's pinched," I said. "It's upwards of thirty-five thousand."

2

The owner of the crunched box accepted my apologies, remembered he was well insured, and decided not to press charges. The policeman sighed, drew a line through his notes, and departed. Jody let down the ramp of his box, brought out Energise, and walked briskly away with him in the direction of the stables. And I returned to my binoculars, took off my battered coat, and went thoughtfully back toward the weighing room.

The peace lasted for all of ten minutes. Until Jody returned from the stables and found I had not canceled my cancellation of his authority to act.

He sought me out among the small crowd standing around talking on the weighing-room veranda.

"Look, Steven," he said. "You've forgotten to tell them I'm still training for you."

He showed no anxiety, just slight exasperation at my oversight. I weakened for one second at the thought of the storm that would undoubtedly break out again, and began to make all the old fatal allowances: he *was* a good trainer, and my horses *did* win, now and again. And I could keep a sharp eye on the bills and let him know I was doing it. And as for the other thing . . . I could easily avoid being robbed in future. . . .

I took a deep breath. It had to be now or never.

19

"I haven't forgotten," I said slowly. "I meant what I said. I'm taking the horses away."

"*What?*"

"I am taking them away."

The naked enmity that filled his face was shocking.

"You *bastard*," he said.

Heads turned again in our direction.

Jody produced several further abusive epithets, all enunciated very clearly in a loud voice. The press notebooks sprouted like mushrooms in little white blobs on the edge of my vision, and I took the only way I knew to shut him up.

"I backed Energise today on the Tote," I said.

Jody said, "So what," very quickly in the second before the impact of what I meant hit him like a punch.

"I'm closing my account with Ganser Mays," I said.

Jody looked absolutely murderous, but he didn't ask *why*. Instead he clamped his jaws together, cast a less welcoming glance to the attentive press, and said very quietly and with menace, "If you say anything, I'll sue you for libel."

"Slander," I said automatically.

"What?"

"Libel is written, slander is spoken."

"I'll have you," he said, "if you say anything."

"Some friendship," I commented.

His eyes narrowed. "It was a pleasure," he said, "to take you for every penny I could."

A small silence developed. I felt that racing had gone thoroughly sour, and that I would never get much fun from it again. Three years of uncomplicated enjoyment had crumbled to disillusionment.

In the end I simply said, "Leave Energise here. I'll fix his transport," and Jody turned on his heel with a stony face and plunged in through the weighing-room door.

*   *   *

The transport proved no problem. I arranged with a young owner-driver of a one-box transport firm that he should take Energise back to his own small transit yard overnight. and ferry him on in a day or two to whichever trainer I decided to send him.

"A dark-brown horse. Almost black," I said. "The gatekeeper will tell you which box he's in. But . . . I don't suppose he'll have a lad with him."

The owner-driver, it developed, could provide a lad to look after Energise. "He'll be right as rain," he said. "No need for you to worry." He had brought two other horses to the course, one of which was in the last race, and he would be away within an hour afterward, he said. We exchanged telephone numbers and addresses and shook hands on the deal.

After that, more out of politeness than through any great appetite for racing, I went back to the private box of the man who had earlier given me lunch, and with whom I'd watched my own horse win.

"Steven, where have you been? We've been waiting to help you celebrate."

Charlie Canterfield, my host, holding his arms wide in welcome, with a glass of champagne in one hand and a cigar in the other. He and his eight or ten other guests sat on dining chairs round a large central table, its white cloth covered now not with the paraphernalia of lunch. but with a jumble of half-full glasses, race cards. binoculars, gloves, handbags, and betting tickets. A faint haze of Havana smoke and the warm smell of alcohol filled the air, and beyond, on the other side of snugly closed glass, lay the balcony overlooking the fresh and windy racecourse.

Four races down and two to go. Midafternoon. Everyone happy in the interval between coffee-and-brandy and cake-and-tea. A cozy little roomful of chat and friendliness and mild social smugness. Well-intentioned people doing no one any harm.

I sighed inwardly and raised a semblance of enjoyment for Charlie's sake, and sipped champagne and listened to everyone telling me it was *great* that Ener-

gise had won. They'd all backed it, they said. "Lots of
lovely lolly, Steven, dear. Such a clever horse . . . and
such a clever little trainer, Jody Leeds."

"Mmm," I said, with a dryness no one heard.

Charlie waved me to the empty chair between him
and a lady in a green hat.

"What do you fancy for the next race?" he asked.

I looked at him with my mind totally blank.

"Can't remember what's running," I said.

Charlie's leisured manner skipped a beat. I'd seen it
in him before, this split-second assessment of a new
factor, and I knew that therein lay the key to his
exceptional business acumen. His body might laze, his
bonhomie might expand like softly whipped cream, but
his brain never took a moment off.

I gave him a twisted smile.

Charlie said, "Come to dinner."

"Tonight, do you mean?"

He nodded.

I bit my thumb and thought about it. "All right."

"Good. Let's say Parkes, Beauchamp Place, eight
o'clock."

"All right."

The relationship between Charlie and me had stood
for years in that vague area between acquaintanceship
and active friendship where chance meetings are enjoyed and deliberate ones seldom arranged. That day
was the first on which he had invited me to his private
box. Asking me for dinner as well meant a basic shift
to new ground.

I guessed he had misread my vagueness, but all the
same I liked him, and no one in his right mind would
pass up a dinner at Parkes. I hoped he wouldn't think
it a wasted evening.

Charlie's guests began disappearing to put bets on
for the next race. I picked up a spare race card that
was lying on the table and knew at once why Charlie
had paid me such acute attention: two of the very top
hurdlers were engaged in battle and the papers had
been talking about it for days.

I looked up and met Charlie's gaze. His eyes were amused.

"Which one, then?" he asked.

"Crepitas."

"Are you betting?"

I nodded. "I did it earlier. On the Tote."

He grunted. "I prefer the bookmakers. I like to know what odds I'm getting before I lay out my cash." And. considering his business was investment banking, that was consistent thinking. "I can't be bothered to walk down, though."

"You can have half of mine, if you like," I said.

"Half of how much?" he said cautiously.

"Ten pounds."

He laughed. "Rumor says you can't think in anything less than three naughts."

"That was an engineering joke," I said, "which escaped."

"How do you mean?"

"I sometimes use a precision lathe. You can just about set it to an accuracy of three naughts—point naught naught naught one. One ten-thousandth of an inch. That's my limit. Can't think in less than three naughts."

He chuckled. "And you never have a thousand on a horse?"

"Oh. I did that, too, once or twice."

He definitely did, that time, hear the arid undertone. I stood up casually and moved toward the glass door to the balcony.

"They're going down to the post," I said.

He came without comment, and we stood outside watching the two stars, Crepitas and Waterboy, bouncing past the stands with their jockeys fighting for control.

Charlie was a shade shorter than I, a good deal stouter. and approximately twenty years older. He wore top-quality clothes as a matter of course, and no one hearing his mellow voice would have guessed his father had been a lorry driver. Charlie had never hidden his origins. Indeed he was justly proud of them. It was simply that under the old educational system he'd been sent to Eton as a local boy on Council money, and had acquired the speech and social habits along with the book learning. His brains had taken him along all his life like a surf rider on the crest of a roller, and it was probably only a modest piece of extra luck that he'd happened to be born within sight of the big school.

His other guests drifted out onto the balcony and claimed his attention. I knew none of them well, most of them by sight, one or two by reputation. Enough for the occasion, not enough for involvement.

The lady in the green hat put a green glove on my arm. "Waterboy looks wonderful, don't you think?"

"Wonderful," I agreed.

She gave me a bright myopic smile from behind thick-lensed glasses. "Could you just tell me what price they're offering now in the ring?"

"Of course."

I raised my binoculars and scanned the boards of the bookmakers ranged in front of a sector of stands lying some way to our right. "It looks like evens Waterboy and five-to-four Crepitas, as far as I can see."

"So kind," said the green lady warmly.

I swung the binoculars round a little to search out Ganser Mays: and there he stood, halfway down the row of bookmakers lining the rails separating the Club Enclosure from Tattersall's, a thin man of middle height with a large sharp nose, steel-rimmed spectacles, and the manner of a High Church clergyman. I had never liked him enough to do more than talk about the weather, but I had trusted him completely, and that had been foolish.

He was leaning over the rails, head bent, talking earnestly to someone in the Club Enclosure, someone hidden from me by a bunch of other people. Then the bunch shifted and moved away, and the person behind them was Jody.

The anger in Jody's body came over sharp and clear, and his lower jaw moved vigorously in speech. Ganser Mays's responses appeared more soothing than fierce, and when Jody finally strode furiously away, Ganser Mays raised his head and looked after him with an expression more thoughtful than actively worried.

Ganser Mays had reached that point in a bookmaker's career where outstanding personal success began to merge into the status of a large and respectable firm. In gamblers' minds he was moving from an individual to an institution. A multiplying host of betting shops bore his name from Glasgow southward, and recently he had announced that next flat season he would sponsor a three-year-old sprint.

He still stood on the rails himself at big meetings to talk to his more affluent customers and keep them faithful. To open his big shark jaws and suck in all the new unwary little fish.

With a wince, I swung my glasses away. I would never know exactly how much Jody and Ganser Mays had stolen from me in terms of cash, but in terms of self-respect they had stripped me of all but crumbs.

The race started, the super-hurdlers battled their hearts out, and Crepitas beat Waterboy by a length. The Tote would pay me a little because of him, and a great deal because of Energise, but two winning bets in one afternoon weren't enough to dispel my depression. I dodged the tea-and-cakes, thanked Charlie for the lunch and said I'd see him later, and went down toward the weighing room again, to see if inspiration would strike in the matter of a choice of trainers.

I heard hurrying footsteps behind me and a hand grabbed my arm.

"Thank goodness I've found you."

He was out of breath and looking worried. The young owner-driver I'd hired for Energise.

"What is it? Box broken down?"

"No. . . . Look, you did say your horse was black, didn't you? I mean, I did get that right, didn't I?"

Anxiety sharpened my voice. "Is there anything wrong with him?"

"No . . . at least not with him, no. But the horse which Mr. Leeds has left for me to take is—well . . . a chestnut mare."

I went with him to the stables. The gatekeeper still smiled with pleasure at things going wrong.

" 'Sright," he said with satisfaction. "Leeds went off a quarter of an hour ago in one of them hire boxes, one horse. Said his own box had had an accident and he was leaving Energise here, instructions of the owner."

"The horse he's left is not Energise," I said.

"Can't help that, can I?" he said virtuously.

I turned to the young man. "Chestnut mare with a big white blaze?"

He nodded.

"That's Asphodel. She ran in the first race today. Jody Leeds trains her. She isn't mine."

"What will I do about her, then?"

"Leave her here," I said. "Sorry about this. Send me a bill for cancellation fees."

He smiled and said he wouldn't, which almost restored my faith in human nature. I thanked him for bothering to find me instead of keeping quiet, taking the wrong horse, and then sending me a bill for work done. He looked shocked that anyone could be so cynical, and I reflected that until I learned from Jody, I wouldn't have been.

Jody had taken Energise after all.

I burned with slow anger, partly because of my own lack of foresight. If he had been prepared to urge Andy-Fred to risk running me down, I should have known that he wouldn't give up at the first setback. He had been determined to get the better of me and whisk Engerise back to his own stable, and I'd underestimated both his bloody-mindedness and his nerve.

I could hardly wait to be free of Jody. I went back to my car and drove away from the racecourse with no thoughts but of which trainer I would ask to take my horses, and how soon I could get them transferred from one to the other.

Charlie smiled across the golden polished wood of the table in Parkes and pushed away his empty coffee cup. His cigar was half smoked, his port half drunk, and his stomach—if mine was anything to go by—full of some of the best food in London.

I wondered what he had looked like as a young man, before the comfortable paunch and the beginning of jowls. Big businessmen were all the better for a little weight, I thought. Lean-and-hungry was for the starters, the hotheads in a hurry. Charlie exuded maturity and wisdom with every excess pound.

He had smooth graying hair, thin on top and brushed back at the sides. Eyes deep set, nose large, mouth firmly straight. Not conventionally a good-looking face, but easy to remember. People who had once met Charlie tended to know him next time.

He had come alone, and the restaurant he had chosen consisted of several smallish rooms with three or four tables in each: a quiet place where privacy was easy. He had talked about racing, food, the Prime Minister, and the state of the stock market, and still had not come to the point.

"I get the impression," he said genially, "that you are waiting for something."

"You've never asked me to dine before."

"I like your company."

"And that's all?"

He tapped ash off the cigar. "Of course not," he said.

"I thought not." I smiled. "But I've probably eaten your dinner under false pretenses."

"Knowingly?"

"Maybe. I don't know exactly what's in your mind."

"Your vagueness," he said. "When someone like you goes into a sort of trance . . ."

"I thought so." I sighed. "Well, that was no useful

productive unawareness of mind; that was just the aftermath of a practically mortal row I'd just had with Jody Leeds."

He sat back in his chair. "What a pity."

"Pity about the row or a pity about the absence of inspiration?"

"Both, I dare say. What was the row about?"

"I gave him the sack."

He stared. "What on earth for?"

"He said if I told anyone that, he'd sue me for slander."

"Oh, did he indeed?" Charlie looked interested all over again, like a horse taking fresh hold of its bit. "And could he?"

"I expect so."

Charlie sucked a mouthful of smoke and trickled it out from one corner of his mouth.

"Care to risk it?" he said.

"Your discretion's better than most. . . ."

"Absolute," he said. "I promise."

I believed him. I said, "He found a way of stealing huge sums from me so that I didn't know I was being robbed."

"But you must have known that *someone* . . ."

I shook my head. "I dare say I'm not the first the trick's been played on. It's so deadly simple."

"Proceed," Charlie said. "You fascinate me."

"Right. Now suppose you are basically a good race-horse trainer but you've got a large and crooked thirst for unearned income."

"I'm supposing," Charlie said.

"First of all, then," I said, "you need a silly mug with a lot of money and enthusiasm and not much knowledge of racing."

"You?" Charlie said.

"Me." I nodded ruefully. "Someone recommends me to you as a good trainer and I'm impressed by your general air of competence and dedication, so I toddle up and ask you if you could find me a good horse, as I'd like to become an owner."

"And do I buy a good horse cheaply and charge you a fortune for it?"

"No. You buy the very best horse you can. I am delighted, and you set about the training, and very soon the horse is ready to run. At this point, you tell me you know a very reliable bookmaker, and you introduce me to him."

"Oh, hmm."

"As you say. The bookmaker, however, is eminently respectable and respected, and as I am not used to betting in large amounts I am glad to be in the hands of so worthy a fellow. You, my trainer, tell me the horse shows great promise, and I might think of a small each-way bet on his first race. A hundred pounds each way, perhaps."

"A small bet!" Charlie exclaimed.

"You point out that that is scarcely more than three weeks' training fees," I said.

"I do?"

"You do. So I gulp a little, as I've always bet in tenners before, and I stake a hundred each way. But, sure enough, the horse does run well and finishes third, and the bookmaker pays out a little instead of me paying him."

I drank the rest of my glass of port. Charlie finished his, and ordered more coffee.

"Next time the horse runs," I went on, "you say it is really well and sure to win, and if I ever want to have a big bet, now's the time, before everyone else jumps on the bandwagon. The bookmaker offers me a good price and I feel euphoric and take the plunge."

"A thousand?"

I nodded. "A thousand."

"And?"

"The word goes round and the horse starts favorite. It is not his day, though. He runs worse than the first time and finishes fifth. You are very upset. You can't understand it. I find myself comforting you and telling you he is bound to run better next time."

"But he doesn't run better next time?"

"But he does. Next time, he wins beautifully."

"But you haven't backed it?"

"Yes, I have. The price this time isn't five-to-two as it was before, but six-to-one. I stake five hundred pounds and win three thousand. I am absolutely delighted. I have regained all the money I had lost and more besides, and I have also gained the prize money for the race. I pay the training bills out of the winnings, and I have recouped part of the purchase price of the horse, and I am very happy with the whole business of being an owner. I ask you to buy me another horse. Buy two or three, if you can find them."

"And this time you get expensive duds?"

"By no means. My second horse is a marvelous two-year-old. He wins his very first race. I have only a hundred on him, mind you, but as it is at ten-to-one, I am still very pleased. So next time out, as my horse is a hot favorite and tipped in all the papers, you encourage me to have a really big bet. Opportunities like this seldom arise, you tell me, as the opposition is hopeless. I am convinced, so I lay out three thousand pounds."

"My God," Charlie said.

"Quite so. My horse sprints out of the stalls and takes the lead like the champion he is and everything is going splendidly. But then, halfway along the five furlongs, a buckle breaks on the saddle and the girths come loose and the jockey has to pull up as best he can, because by now he is falling off."

"Three thousand!" Charlie said.

"All gone." I nodded. "You are unconsolable. The strap was new, the buckle faulty. Never mind, I say kindly, gulping hard. Always another day."

"And there is?"

"You're learning. Next time out, the horse is favorite again and I have five hundred on. He wins, all right, and although I have not this time won back all I lost— well, it's the second time the horse has brought home a decent prize and, taking all in all, I am not out of pocket, and I have had a great deal of pleasure and excitement. And I am well content."

"And so it goes on?"

"And so, indeed, it goes on. I find I get more and more delight from watching horses. I get particular delight if the horses are my own, and although in time, of course, my hobby costs me a good deal of money, because owners on the whole don't make a profit, I am totally happy and consider it well spent."

"And then what happens?"

"Nothing really," I said. "I just begin to get these niggling suspicions and I thrust them out of my head and think how horribly disloyal I am being to you, after all the winners you have trained for me. But the suspicions won't lie down. . . . I've noticed, you see, that when I have my biggest bets, my horses don't win."

"A lot of owners could say the same," Charlie said.

"Oh, sure. But I tot up all the big bets which didn't come up, and they come to nearly forty thousand pounds."

"Good God."

"I am really ashamed of myself, but I begin to *wonder*. I say to myself, suppose—just suppose— that every time I stake anything over a thousand, my trainer and my bookmaker conspire together and simply keep the money, and make sure my horse doesn't win. Just suppose that if I stake three thousand, they split if fifty-fifty, and the horse runs badly, or is left, or the buckle on the girth breaks. Just suppose the next time out my horse is trained to the utmost and the race is carefully chosen and he duly wins, and I am delighted. . . . Just suppose that this time my bookmaker and my trainer are betting on the horse themselves . . . with the money they stole from me last time."

Charlie looked riveted.

"If my horse wins, they win. If my horse loses, they haven't lost their own money, but only mine."

"Neat."

"Yes. So the weeks pass and now the flat season is

finished, and we are back again with the jumpers. And you, my trainer, have found and bought for me a beautiful young hurdler, a really top-class horse. I back him a little in his first race and he wins it easily. I am thrilled. I am also worried, because you tell me there is a race absolutely made for him at Sandown Park which he is certain to win, and you encourage me to have a very big bet on him. I am by now filled with horrid doubts and fears, and as I particularly admire this horse I do not want his heart broken by trying to win when he isn't allowed to . . . which I am sure happened to one or two of the others. So I say I will not back him."

"Unpopular?"

"Very. You press me harder than ever before to lay out a large stake. I refuse. You are obviously annoyed, and warn me that the horse will win and I will be sorry. I say I'll wait till next time. You say I am making a big mistake."

"When do I say all this?"

"Yesterday."

"And today?" Charlie asked.

"Today I am suffering from suspicion worse than ever. Today I think that maybe you will let the horse win if he can, just to prove I was wrong not to back him, so that next time you will have no difficulty at all in persuading me to have a bigger bet than ever."

"Tut, tut."

"Yes. So today I don't tell you that a little while ago—because of my awful doubts—I opened a credit account with the Tote, and today I also don't tell you that I have backed my horse for a thousand pounds on my credit account."

"Deceitful of you."

"Certainly."

"And your horse wins," Charlie said, nodding.

"He looked superb." I smiled wryly. "You tell me after the race that it is my own fault I didn't back him. You say you did try to get me to. You say I'd do better to take your advice next time."

"And then?"

"Then," I said, sighing, "all the weeks of suspicion just jelled into certainty. I knew he'd been cheating me in other ways, too. Little ways. Little betrayals of friendship. Nothing enormous. I told him there wasn't going to be a next time. I said I would be taking the horses away."

"What did he say too that?"

"He didn't ask why."

"Oh, dear," Charlie said.

3

I told Charlie everything that had happened that day. All amusement died from his expression, and by the end he was looking grim.

"He'll get away with it," he said finally.

"Oh, yes."

"You remember, I suppose, that his father's a member of the Jockey Club?"

"Yes."

"Above suspicion, is Jody Leeds."

Jody's father, Quintus Leeds, had achieved pillar-of-the-Turf status by virtue of being born the fifth son of a sporting peer, owning a few race horses, and having the right friends. He had a physically commanding presence, tall, large, and handsome, and his voice and handshake radiated firm confidence. He was apt to give people straight piercing looks from fine gray eyes, and to purse his mouth thoughtfully and shake his head as if pledged to secrecy when asked for an opinion. I privately thought his appearance and mannerisms were a lot of glossy window dressing concealing a marked absence of goods, but there was no doubting that he was basically well-meaning and honest.

He was noticeably proud of Jody, puffing up his chest and beaming visibly in unsaddling enclosures from Epsom to York.

In his father's eyes, Jody, energetic, capable, and

clever, could do no wrong. Quintus would believe in him implicitly, and for all his suspect shortness of intelligence, he carried enough weight to sway official opinion.

As Jody had said, I couldn't prove a thing. If I so much as hinted at theft, he'd slap a lawsuit on me, and the bulk of the Jockey Club would be ranged on his side.

"What will you do?" Charlie said.

"Don't know." I half smiled. "Nothing, I suppose."

"It's bloody unfair."

"All crime is bloody unfair on the victim."

Charlie made a face at the general wickedness of the world and called for the bill.

Outside we turned left and walked down Beauchamp Place together, having both, as it happened, parked our cars round the corner in Walton Street. The night was cold, cloudy, dry, and still windy. Charlie pulled his coat collar up round his ears and put on thick black leather gloves.

"I hate the winter," he said.

"I don't mind it."

"You're young," he said. "You don't feel the cold."

"Not that young. Thirty-five."

"Practically a baby."

We turned the corner and the wind bit sharply with arctic teeth. "I hate it," Charlie said.

His car, a big blue Rover 3500, was parked nearer than my Lamborghini. We stopped beside his, and he unlocked the door. Down the street, a girl in a long skirt walked in our direction, the wind blowing her skirt sidewise and her hair like flags.

"Very informative evening," he said, holding out his hand.

"Not what you expected, though," I said, shaking it.

"Better, perhaps."

He opened his door and began to lower himself into

the driver's seat. The girl in the long skirt walked past us, her heels brisk on the pavement. Charlie fastened his seat belt and I shut his door.

The girl stopped hesitated, and turned back.

"Excuse me," she said. "But I wonder . . ." She stopped, appearing to think better of it.

"Can we help you?" I said.

She was American, in her early twenties, and visibly cold. Round her shoulders she wore only a thin silk shawl, and under that a thin silk shirt. No gloves. Gold sandals. A small gold mesh purse. In the streetlights her skin looked blue, and she was shivering violently.

"Get in my car," Charlie suggested, winding down his window. "Out of the wind."

She shook her head. "I guess . . ." She began to turn away.

"Don't be silly," I said. "You need help. Accept it."

"But . . ."

"Tell us what you need."

She said with a rush, "I need some money."

"Is that all?" I said, and fished out my wallet. "How much?"

"Enough for a taxi . . . to Hampstead."

I held out a fiver. "That do?"

"Yes. I . . . Where shall I send it back to?"

"Don't bother."

"But I must."

Charlie said, "He's got wads of the stuff. He won't miss it."

"That's not the point," the girl said. "If you won't tell me how to repay it, I can't take it."

"It is ridiculous to argue about morals when you're freezing," I said. "My name is Steven Scott. Address, Regent's Park Malthouse. That'll find me."

"Thanks."

"I'll drive you, if you like. I have my car." I pointed along the street.

"No, thanks," she said. "How d'you think I got *into* this mess?"

"How, then?"

She pulled the thin shawl close. "I accepted a simple invitation to dinner and found there were strings attached. So I left him at the soup stage and blasted out, and it was only when I was walking away that I realized that I'd no money with me. He'd collected me, you see." She smiled suddenly, showing straight white teeth. "Some girls are dumber than others."

"Let Steven go and find you a taxi, then," Charlie said.

"Okay."

It took me several minutes, but she was still huddled against the outside of Charlie's car, sheltering as best she could from the worst of the wind, when I got back. I climbed out of the taxi and she climbed in, and without more ado drove away.

"A fool and his money," Charlie said.

"That was no con trick."

"It would be a good one," he said. "How do you know she's not hopping out of the cab two blocks away and shaking a fiver out of the next Sir Galahad?"

He laughed, wound up the window, waved, and pointed his Rover toward home.

Monday morning brought the good news and the bad.

The good was a letter with a five-pound note enclosed. Sucks to Charlie, I thought.

Dear Mr. Scott,

I was so grateful for your help on Saturday night. I guess I'll never go out on a date again without the cab fare home.

Yours sincerely,
Alexandra Ward

The bad news was in public print: comments in both newspapers delivered to my door (one sporting, one ordinary) about the disloyalty of owners who shed their hard-working trainers. One said:

> Particularly hard on Jody Leeds that after all he had done for Mr. Scott, the owner should see fit to announce he would be sending his horses elsewhere. As we headlined in this column a year ago, Jody Leeds took on the extensive Berksdown Court Stables especially to house the expanding Scott string. Now without as much as half an hour's warning, the twenty-eight-year-old trainer is left flat, with all his new liabilities still outstanding. Treachery may sound a harsh word. Ingratitude is not.

And the other, in more tabloid vein:

> Leeds (28), smarting from the sack delivered by ungrateful owner Steven Scott (35), said at Sandown on Saturday, "I am right in the cart now. Scott dumped me while still collecting backslaps for the win on his hurdler Energise, which I trained. I am sick at heart. You sweat your guts out for an owner, and he kicks you in the teeth."
>
> High time trainers were protected from this sort of thing. Rumour has it Leeds may sue.

All those press notebooks, all those extended press ears had not been there for nothing. Very probably they did all genuinely believe that Jody had had a raw deal, but not one single one had bothered to ask what the view looked like from where I stood. Not a single one seemed to think that there might have been an overpowering reason for my action.

I disgustedly put down both papers, finished my breakfast, and settled down to the day's work, which,

as usual, consisted mostly of sitting still in an armchair
and staring vacantly into space.

Around midafternoon, stiff and chilly, I wrote to
Miss Ward.

Dear Miss Ward,

Thank you very much for the fiver. Will you
have dinner with me? No strings attached. I enclose five pounds for the cab fare home.

Yours sincerely,
Steven Scott

In the evening, I telephoned three different race-
horse trainers and offered them three horses each.
They all accepted, but with the reservations blowing
cool in their voices. None actually asked why I had
split with Jody, though all had obviously read the
papers.

One, a blunt North Countryman, said, "I'll want a
guarantee you'll leave them with me for at least six
months, so long as they don't go lame or something."

"All right."

"In writing."

"If you like."

"Aye, I do like. You send 'em up with a guarantee
and I'll take 'em."

For Energise, I picked a large yard in Sussex where
hurdlers did especially well, and under the guarded
tones of the trainer, Rupert Ramsey, I could hear that
he thought almost as much of the horses as I did.

For the last three, I chose Newmarket, a middle-
sized stable of average achievement. No single basket
would ever again contain all the Scott eggs.

Finally, with a grimace, I picked up the receiver and
dialed Jody's familiar number. It was not he who answered, however, but Felicity, his wife.

Her voice was sharp and bitter. "What do you
want?"

I pictured her in their luxuriously furnished drawing room, a thin positive blond girl, every bit as competent and hard-working as Jody. She would be wearing tight blue jeans and an expensive shirt, there would be six gold bracelets jingling on her wrist, and she would smell of a musk-based scent. She held intolerant views on most things and stated them forthrightly, but she had never, before that evening, unleashed on me personally the scratchy side of her mind.

"To talk about transport," I said.

"So you really are kicking our props away."

"You'll survive."

"That's bloody complacent claptrap," she said angrily. "I could kill you. After all Jody's done for you."

I paused. "Did he tell you why I'm breaking with him?"

"Some stupid little quarrel about ten quid on a bill."

"It's a great deal more than that," I said.

"Rubbish."

"Ask him," I said. "In any case, three horse boxes will collect my horses on Thursday morning. The drivers will know which ones each of them has to take and where to take them. You tell Jody that if he mixes them up he can pay the bills for sorting them out."

The names she called me would have shaken Jody's father to the roots.

"Thursday," I said. "Three horse boxes, different destinations. And goodbye."

No pleasure in it. None at all.

I sat gloomily watching a play on television and hearing hardly a word. At nine-forty-five, the telephone interrupted, and I switched off.

". . . Just want to know, sir, where I stand."

Raymond Child. Jump jockey. Middle-ranker, thirty years old, short on personality. He rode competently enough, but the longer I went racing and the more I learned, the more I could see his shortcomings. I was certain also that Jody could not have manipulated my horses quite so thoroughly without help at the wheel.

"I'll send you an extra present for Energise," I said. Jockeys were paid an official percentage of the winning prize money through a central system, but especially grateful owners occasionally came across with more.

"Thank you, sir." He sounded surprised.

"I had a good bet on him."

"Did you, sir?" The surprise was extreme. "But Jody said—" He stopped dead.

"I backed him on the Tote."

"Oh."

The silence lengthened. He cleared his throat. I waited.

"Well, sir. Er . . . about the future . . ."

"I'm sorry," I said, half meaning it. "I'm grateful for the winners you've ridden. I'll send you the present for Energise. But in the future he'll be ridden by the jockey attached to his new stable."

This time there was no tirade of bad language. This time, just a slow defeated sigh and the next best thing to an admission.

"Can't really blame you, I suppose."

He disconnected before I could reply.

Tuesday I should have had a runner at Chepstow, over on the west side of the Bristol Channels, but since I'd canceled Jody's authority he couldn't send it. I stayed in my rooms unproductively all morning and in the afternoon walked from Kensington Gardens to the Tower of London. Cold gray damp air, with seagulls making a racket over the low-tide mud. Coffee-colored river racing down on the last of the ebb. I stood looking toward the City from the top of little Tower Hill, and thought of all the lives that had ended there under the axe. December mood, through and through. I bought a bag of roasted chestnuts and went home by bus.

Wednesday brought a letter.

Dear Mr. Scott,

When and where?

Alexandra Ward

She had kept the five-pound note.

On Thursday evening, the three new trainers confirmed that they had received the expected horses, on Friday I did a little work, and on Saturday I drove down to Cheltenham races. I had not, it was true, exactly expected a rousing cheer, but the depth and extent of the animosity shown to me was acutely disturbing.

Several backs were turned, not ostentatiously but decisively. Several acquaintances lowered their eyes in embarrassment when talking to me, and hurried away as soon as possible. The press looked speculative, the trainers wary, and the Jockey Club coldly hostile.

Charlie Canterfield alone came up with a broad smile and shook me vigorously by the hand.

"Have I come out in spots?" I said.

He laughed. "You've kicked the underdog. The British never forgive it."

"Even when the underdog bites first?"

"Underdogs are never in the wrong."

He led me away to the bar. "I've been taking a small poll for you. Ten percent think it would be fair to hear your side. Ten percent think you ought to be shot. What will you drink?"

"Scotch. No ice or water. What about the other eighty percent?"

"Enough righteous indignation to keep the Mother's Union going for months." He paid for the drinks. "Cheers."

"And to you, too."

"It'll blow over," Charlie said.

"I guess so."

"What do you fancy in the third?"

We discussed the afternoon's prospects and didn't refer again to Jody, but later, alone, I found it hard to ignore the general climate. I backed a couple of horse's on the Tote for a tenner each, and lost. That sort of day.

All afternoon I was fiercely tempted to protest that it was I who was the injured party, not Jody. Then I thought of the further thousands he would undoubtedly screw out of me in damages if I opened my mouth, and I kept it shut.

The gem of the day was Quintus himself, who planted his great frame solidly in my path and told me loudly that I was a bloody disgrace to the good name of racing. Quintus, I reflected, so often spoke in clichés.

"I'll tell you something," he said. "You would have been elected to the Jockey Club if you hadn't served Jody such a dirty trick. Your name was up for consideration. You won't be invited now, I'll see to that."

He gave me a short curt nod and stepped aside. I didn't move.

"Your son is the one for dirty tricks."

"How dare you!"

"You'd best believe it."

"Absolute nonsense. The discrepancy on your bill was a simple secretarial mistake. If you try to say it was anything else—"

"I know," I said. "He'll sue."

"Quite right. He has a right to every penny he can get."

I walked away. Quintus might be biased, but I knew I'd get a straight answer from the press.

I asked the senior columnist of a leading daily, a fiftyish man who wrote staccato prose and sucked peppermints to stop himself smoking.

"What reason is Jody Leeds giving for losing my horses?"

The columnist sucked and breathed out a gust of sweetness.

"Says he charged you by mistake for some schooling Raymond Child didn't do."

"That all?"

"Says you accused him of stealing and were changing your trainer."

"And what's your reaction to that?"

"I haven't got one." He shrugged and sucked contemplatively. "Others . . . The concensus seems to be it was a genuine mistake and you've been unreasonable— to put it mildly."

"I see," I said. "Thanks."

"Is that all? No story?"

"No," I said. "Sorry."

He put another peppermint in his mouth, nodded noncommittally, and turned away to more fertile prospects. As far as he was concerned, I was last week's news. Others, this Saturday, were up for the chop.

I walked thoughtfully down on the Club lawn to watch the next race. It really was not much fun being cast as everyone's villain, and the clincher was delivered by a girl I'd once taken to Ascot.

"Steven, dear," she said with coquettish reproof, "you're a big rich bully. That poor boy's struggling to make ends meet. Even if he did pinch a few quid off you, why get into such a tizz? So uncool, don't you think?"

"You believe the rich should lie down for Robin Hood?"

"What?"

"Never mind."

I gave it up and went home.

The evening was a great deal better. At eight o'clock, I collected Miss Alexandra Ward from an address in Hampstead and took her to dinner in the red-and-gold grillroom of the Café Royal.

Seen again in kinder light, properly warm, and not blown to rags by the wind, she was everything last week's glimpse had suggested. She wore the same long black skirt, the same cream shirt, the same cream silk shawl. Also the gold sandals, gold mesh purse, and no gloves. But her brown hair was smooth and shining, her skin glowing, her eyes bright, and over all lay the indefinable extra, a typically American brand of grooming.

She opened the door herself when I rang the bell, and for an appreciable pause we simply looked at each other. What she saw was, I supposed, about six feet of solidly built chap, dark hair, dark eyes, no warts to speak of. Tidy, clean, house-trained, and dressed in a conventional dinner jacket.

"Good evening," I said.

She smiled, nodded as if endorsing a decision, stepped out through the door, and pulled it shut behind her.

"My sister lives here," she said, indicating the house. "I'm on a visit. She's married to an Englishman."

I opened the car door for her. She sat smoothly inside, and I started the engine and drove off.

"A visit from the States?" I asked.

"Yes. From Westchester . . . outside New York."

"Executive ladder-climbing country?" I said, smiling.

She gave me a quick sidewise glance. "You know Westchester?"

"No. Been to New York a few times, that's all."

We stopped at some traffic lights. She remarked that it was a fine night. I agreed.

"Are you married?" she said abruptly.

"Did you bring the fiver?"

"Yes, I did."

"Well . . . No, I'm not."

The light changed to green. We drove on.

"Are you truthful?" she said.

"In that respect, yes. Not married now. Never have been."

"I like to know," she said with mild apology.

"I don't blame you."

"For the sakes of the wives."

"Yes."

I pulled up in due course in front of the Café Royal at Piccadilly Circus, and helped her out of the car. As we went in, she looked back and saw a small thin man taking my place in the driving seat.

"He works for me," I said. "He'll park the car."

She looked amused. "He waits around to do that?"

"On overtime, Saturday nights."

"So he likes it?"

"Begs me to take out young ladies. Other times I do my own parking."

In the full light inside the hall, she stopped for another straight look at what she'd agreed to dine with.

"What do you expect of me?" she said.

"Before I collected you, I expected honesty, directness, and prickles. Now that I've known you for half an hour, I expect prickles, directness, and honesty."

She smiled widely, the white teeth shining and little pouches of fun swelling her lower eyelids.

"That isn't what I meant."

"No . . . So what do you expect of me?"

"Thoroughly gentlemanly conduct and a decent dinner."

"How dull."

"Take it or leave it."

"The bar," I said, pointing, "is over there. I take it."

She gave me another flashing smile, younger sister to the first, and moved where I'd said. She drank vodka martini, I drank Scotch, and we both ate a few black olives and spat out the stones genteelly into our fists.

"Do you usually pick up girls in the street?" she said.

"Only when they fall."

"Fallen girls?"

I laughed. "Not those, no."

"What do you do for a living?"

I took a mouthful of Scotch. "I'm a sort of engineer." It sounded boring.

"Bridges and things?"

"Nothing so permanent or important."

"What, then?"

I smiled wryly. "I make toys."

"You make . . . *what?*"

"Toys. Things to play with."

"I know what toys are, damn it."

"What do you do?" I asked. "In Westchester."

She gave me an amused glance over her glass. "You take it for granted that I work?"

"You have the air."

"I cook, then."

"Hamburgers and French fries?"

Her eyes gleamed. "Weddings and stuff. Parties."

"A lady caterer."

She nodded. "With a girl friend. Millie."

"When do you go back?"

"Thursday."

Thursday suddenly seemed rather close. After a noticeable pause, she added almost defensively, "It's Christmas, you see. We've a lot of work then, and around New Year's. Millie couldn't do it all alone."

"Of course not."

We went in to dinner and ate smoked trout and steak wrapped in pastry. She read the menu from start to finish with professional interest and checked with the headwaiter the ingredients of two or three dishes.

"So many things are different over here," she explained.

She knew little about wine. "I guess I drink it when I'm given it, but I've a better palate for spirits." The wine waiter looked skeptical, but she wiped that look off his face later by correctly identifying the brandy he brought with the coffee as Armagnac.

"Where is your toy factory?" she asked.

"I don't have a factory."

"But you said you made toys."

"Yes, I do."

She looked disbelieving. "You don't mean you actually *make* them. I mean, with your own hands?"

I smiled. "Yes."

"But . . ." She looked round the velvety room with the thought showing as clear as spring water: if I worked with my hands, how could I afford such a place?

"I don't often make them," I said. "Most of the time I go to the races."

"Okay," she said. "I give in. You've got me hooked. Explain the mystery."

"Have some more coffee."

"Mr. Scott . . ." She stopped. "That sounds silly, doesn't it?"

"Yes, Miss Ward, it does."

"Steven . . ."

"Much better."

"My mother calls me Alexandra, Millie calls me Al. Take your pick."

"Allie?"

"For God's sakes."

"I invent toys," I said. "I patent them. Other people manufacture them. I collect royalties."

"Oh."

"Does 'oh' mean enlightenment, fascination, or boredom to death?"

"It means, oh, how extraordinary; oh, how interesting; and, oh, I never knew people did things like that."

"Quite a lot do."

"Did you invent Monopoly?"

I laughed. "Unfortunately not."

"But that sort of thing?"

"Mechanical toys, mostly."

"How odd . . ." She stopped, thinking better of saying what was in her mind. I knew the reaction well, so I finished the sentence for her.

"How odd for a grown man to spend his life in toyland?"

"You said it."

"Children's minds have to be fed."

She considered it. "And the next bunch of leaders are children today?"

"You rate it too high. The next lot of parents, teachers, louts, and layabouts are children today."

"And you are fired with missionary zeal?"

"All the way to the bank."

"Cynical."

"Better than pompous."

"More honest," she agreed. Her eyes smiled in the soft light, half mocking, half friendly, greeny-gray and shining, the whites ultra-white. There was nothing wrong with the design of her eyebrows. Her nose was short and straight, her mouth curved up at the corners, and her cheeks had faint hollows in the right places. Assembled, the components added up not to a standard type of beauty, but to a face of character and vitality. Part of the story written, I thought. Lines of good fortune, none of discontent. No anxiety, no inner confusion. A good deal of self-assurance, knowing she looked attractive and had succeeded in the job she'd chosen. Definitely not a virgin: a girl's eyes were always different, after.

"Are all your days busy," I asked, "between now and Thursday?"

"There are some minutes here and there."

"Tomorrow?"

She smiled and shook her head. "Not a chink tomorrow. Monday . . . if you like."

"I'll collect you," I said. "Monday morning, at ten."

4

Rupert Ramsey's voice on the telephone sounded resigned rather than welcoming.

"Yes, of course, do come down to see your horses, if you'd like to. Do you know the way?"

He gave me directions that proved easy to follow, and at eleven-thirty Sunday morning, I drove through his white-painted stone gateposts and drew up in the large graveled area before his house.

He lived in a genuine Georgian house, simple in design, with large airy rooms and elegant plasterwork ceilings. Nothing self-consciously antique about the furnishings: all periods mingled together in a working atmosphere that was wholly modern.

Rupert himself was about forty-five, intensely energetic under a misleadingly languid exterior. His voice drawled slightly. I knew him only by sight, and it was to all intents the first time we had met.

"How do you do?" He shook hands. "Care to come into my office?"

I followed him through the white front door, across the large square hall, and into the room he called his office, but which was furnished entirely as a sitting room except for a dining table that served as a desk, and a gray filing cabinet in one corner.

"Do sit down." He indicated an armchair. "Cigarette?"

"Don't smoke."

"Wise man." He smiled as if he didn't really think so, and lit one for himself.

"Energise," he said, "is showing signs of having had a hard race."

"But he won easily," I said.

"It looked that way, certainly." He inhaled, breathing out through his nose. "All the same, I'm not too happy about him."

"In what way?"

"He needs building up. We'll do it, don't you fear. But he looks a bit thin at present."

"How about the other two?"

"Dial's jumping out of his skin. Ferryboat needs a lot of work yet."

"I don't think Ferryboat likes racing any more."

The cigarette paused on its way to his mouth.

"Why do you say that?" he asked.

"He's had three races this autumn. . . . I expect you'll have looked up his form. He's run badly every time. Last year he was full of enthusiasm and won three times out of seven starts, but the last of them took a lot of winning . . . and Raymond Child cut him raw with his whip. And during the summer out at grass Ferryboat seems to have decided that if he gets too near the front he's in for a beating, so it's only good sense *not* to get near the front, and he consequently isn't trying."

He drew deeply on the cigarette, giving himself time.

"Do you expect me to get better results than Jody?"

"With Ferryboat, or in general?"

"Let's say both."

I smiled. "I don't expect much from Ferryboat. Dial's a novice, an unknown quantity. Energise might win the Champion Hurdle."

"You didn't answer my question," he said pleasantly.

"No . . . I expect you to get different results from Jody. Will that do?"

"I'd very much like to know why you left him."

"Disagreements over money," I said. "Not over the way he trained the horses."

He tapped ash off with the precision that meant his mind was elsewhere. When he spoke, it was slowly.

"Were you always satisfied with the way your horses ran?"

The question hovered delicately in the air, full of inviting little traps. He looked up suddenly and met my eyes, and his own widened with comprehension. "I see you understand what I'm asking."

"Yes. But I can't answer. Jody says he will sue me for slander if I tell people why I left him, and I've no reason to doubt him."

"That remark in itself is a slander."

"Indubitably."

He got cheerfully to his feet and stubbed out the cigarette. A good deal more friendliness seeped into his manner.

"Right, then. Let's go out and look at your horses."

We went out into his yard, which showed prosperity at every turn. The thin cold December sun shone on fresh paint, wall-to-wall tarmac, tidy flower tubs and well-kept stable lads. There was none of the clutter I was accustomed to at Jody's: no brooms leaning against walls, no rugs, rollers, brushes, and bandages lying in ready heaps, no straggles of hay across the swept ground. Jody liked to give owners the impression that work was being done, that care for the horses was nonstop. Rupert, it seemed, preferred to tuck the sweat and toil out of sight. At Jody's, the muck heap was always with you. At Rupert's, it was invisible.

"Dial is here. . . ."

We stopped at a box along a row outside the main quadrangle, and with an unobtrusive flick of his fingers Rupert summoned a lad hovering twenty feet away.

"This is Donny," he said. "Looks after Dial."

I shook hands with Donny, a young tough-looking boy of about twenty with unsmiling eyes and a you-can't-con-me expression. From the look he directed first at Rupert and then later at the horse, I gathered that this was his overall attitude to life, not an announcement of no confidence in me personally. When we'd looked at and admired the robust little chestnut, I tried Donny with a fiver. It raised a nod of thanks, but no smile.

Further along the same row stood Ferryboat, looking out on the world with a lackluster eye and scarcely shifting from one leg to the other when we went into his box. His lad, in contrast to Donny, gave him an indulgent smile, and accepted his gift from me with a beam.

"Energise is in the main yard," Rupert said, leading the way. "Across in the corner."

When we were halfway there, two other cars rolled up the drive and disgorged a collection of men in sheepskin coats and ladies in furs and jangly bracelets. They saw Rupert and waved and began to stream into the yard.

Rupert said, "I'll show you Energise in just a moment."

"It's all right," I said. "You tell me which box he's in. I'll look at him myself. You see to your other owners."

"Number Fourteen, then. I'll be with you again shortly."

I nodded and walked on to No. 14. Unbolted the door. Went in. The near-black horse was tied up inside. Ready, I supposed, for my visit.

Horse and I looked at each other. My old friend, I thought. The only one of all of them with whom I'd ever had any real contact. I talked to him, as in the horse box, looking guiltily over my shoulder at the open door for fear someone should hear me and think me nuts.

I could see at once why Rupert had been unhappy about him. He looked thinner. All that crashing about in the horse box could have done him no good.

Across the yard I could see Rupert talking to the

newcomers and shepherding them to their horses. Owners came en masse on Sunday mornings.

I was content to stay where I was. I spent probably twenty minutes with Energise, and he instilled in me some very strange ideas.

Rupert came back hurrying and apologizing. "You're still here. . . . I'm so sorry."

"Don't be," I assured him.

"Come into the house for a drink."

"I'd like to."

We joined the other owners and returned to his office for lavish issues of gin and Scotch. Drinks for visiting owners weren't allowable as a business expense for tax purposes unless the visiting owners were foreign. Jody had constantly complained of it to all and sundry while accepting cases of the stuff from me with casual nods. Rupert poured generously and dropped no hints, and I found it a refreshing change.

The other owners were excitedly making plans for the Christmas meeting at Kempton Park. Rupert made introductions, explaining that Energise, too, was due to run there in the Christmas Hurdle.

"After the way he won at Sandown," remarked one of the sheepskin coats, "he must be a cast-iron certainty."

I glanced at Rupert for an opinion, but he was busy with bottles and glasses.

"I hope so," I said.

The sheepskin coat nodded sagely.

His wife, a cozy-looking lady who had shed her ocelot and now stood five-feet-nothing in bright-orange wool, looked from him to me in puzzlement.

"But, George, honey, Energise is trained by that nice young man with the pretty little wife. You know, the one who introduced us to Ganser Mays."

She smiled happily and appeared not to notice the poleaxed state of her audience. I must have stood immobile for almost a minute while the implications fizzed around my brain, and during that time the conversation between George, honey, and the bright-orange wool had flowed on into the chances of their own chaser in a later race. I dragged them back.

"Excuse me," I said, "but I didn't catch your names. . . ."

"George Vine," said the sheepskin coat, holding out a chunky hand. "And my wife, Poppet."

"Steven Scott," I said.

"Glad to know you." He gave his empty glass to Rupert, who amiably refilled it with gin and tonic. "Poppet doesn't read the racing news much, so she wouldn't know you've left Jody Leeds."

"Did you say," I asked carefully, "that Jody Leeds introduced you to Ganser Mays?"

"Oh, no," Poppet said, smiling. "His wife did."

"That's right." George nodded. "Bit of luck."

"You see," Poppet explained conversationally, "the prices on the Tote are sometimes so awfully small and it's all such a lottery, isn't it? I mean, you never know really what you're going to get for your money, like you do with the bookies."

"Is that what she said?" I asked.

"Who? Oh . . . Jody Leeds's wife. Yes, that's right, she did. I'd just been picking up my winnings on one of our horses from the Tote, you see, and she was doing the same at the next window—the Late-Pay window, that was—and she said what a shame it was that the Tote was only paying three-to-one when the bookies' starting price was five-to-one, and I absolutely agreed with her, and we just sort of stood there chatting. I told her that only last week we had bought the steeplechaser which had just won, and it was our first ever race horse, and she was so interested and explained that she was a trainer's wife and that sometimes when she got tired of the Tote paying out so little she bet with a bookie. I said I didn't like pushing along the rows with all those men shoving and shouting and she laughed and said she meant one on the rails, so you could just walk up to them and not go through to the bookies' enclosure at all. But of course you have to know them—I mean, they have to know *you*, if you see what I mean. And neither George nor I knew any of them, as I explained to Mrs. Leeds."

She stopped to take a sip of her drink. I listened in fascination.

"Well," she went on, "Mrs. Leeds sort of hesitated and then I got this great idea of asking her if she could possibly introduce us to *her* bookie on the rails."

"And she did?"

"She thought it was a great idea."

She would.

"So we collected George and she introduced us to dear Ganser Mays. And," she finished triumphantly, "he gives us much better odds than the Tote."

George Vine nodded several times in agreement.

"Trouble is," he said, "you know what wives are— she bets more than ever."

"George, honey." A token protest only.

"You know you do, love."

"It isn't worth doing in sixpences," she said, smiling. "You never win enough that way."

He patted her fondly on the shoulder and said man-to-man to me, "When Ganser Mays's account comes every month, if she's won, she takes the winnings, and if she's lost, I pay."

Poppet smiled happily. "George, honey, you're sweet."

"Which do you do most?" I asked her. "Win or lose?"

She made a face. "Now that's a naughty question, Mr. Scott."

Next morning, ten o'clock to the second, I collected Allie from Hampstead.

Seen in daylight for the first time, she was sparkling as the day was rotten. I arrived at her door with a big black umbrella holding off slanting sleet, and she opened the door in a neat white mackintosh and knee-high black boots. Her hair bounced with new washing, and the bloom on her skin had nothing to do with Max Factor.

I tried a gentlemanly kiss on the cheek. She smelled of fresh flowers and bath soap.

"Good morning," I said.

She chuckled. "You English are so formal."

"Not always."

She sheltered under the umbrella down the path to the car and sat inside with every glossy hair dry and in place.

"Where are we going?"

"Fasten your lap straps," I said. "To Newmarket."

"Newmarket?"

"To look at horses." I let in the clutch and pointed the Lamborghini roughly northeast.

"I might have guessed."

I grinned. "Is there anything you'd really rather do?"

"I've visited three museums, four picture galleries, six churches, one Tower of London, two Houses of Parliament, and seven theatres."

"In how long?"

"Sixteen days."

"High time you saw some real life."

The white teeth flashed. "If you'd lived with my two small nephews for sixteen days, you couldn't wait to get away from it."

"Your sister's children?"

She nodded. "Ralph and William. Little devils."

"What do they play with?"

She was amused. "The toymaker's market research?"

"The customer is always right."

We crossed the North Circular road and took the A-1 toward Baldock.

"Ralph dresses up a doll in soldier's uniforms, and William makes forts on the stairs and shoots dried beans at anyone going up."

"Healthy aggressive stuff."

"When I was little, I hated being given all those

educational things that were supposed to be good for you."

I smiled. "It's well known there are two sorts of toys: the ones that children like and the ones their mothers buy. Guess which there are more of?"

"You're cynical."

"So I'm often told," I said. "It isn't true."

The wipers worked overtime against the sleet on the windshield, and I turned up the heater. She sighed with what appeared to be contentment. The car purred easily across Cambridgeshire and into Suffolk, and the ninety-minute journey seemed short.

It wasn't the best of weather, but even in July the stable I'd chosen for my three young flat racers would have looked depressing. There were two smallish quadrangles side by side, built tall and solid in Edwardian brick. All the doors were painted a dead dull dark brown. No decorations, no flowers, no grass, no gaiety of spirit in the whole place.

Like many Newmarket yards, it led straight off the street and was surrounded by houses. Allie looked around without enthusiasm and put into words exactly what I was thinking.

"It looks more like a prison."

Bars on the windows of the boxes. Solid ten-foot-tall gates at the road entrance. Jagged glass set in concrete along the top of the boundary wall. Padlocks swinging on every bolt on every door in sight. All that was missing was a uniformed figure with a gun, and maybe they had those, too, on occasion.

The master of all this security proved pretty dour himself. Trevor Kennet shook hands with a smile that looked an unaccustomed effort for the muscles involved, and invited us into the stable office out of the rain.

A bare room: linoleum, scratched metal furniture, strip lighting, and piles of paperwork. The contrast between this and the grace of Rupert Ramsey was remarkable. A pity I had taken Allie to the wrong one.

"They've settled well, your horses." His voice dared me to disagree.

"Splendid," I said mildly.

"You'll want to see them, I expect."

As I'd come from London to do so, I felt his remark silly.

"They're doing no work yet, of course."

"No," I agreed. The last flat season had finished six weeks ago. The next lay some three months ahead. No owner in his senses would have expected his flat horses to be in full work in December. Trevor Kennet had a genius for the obvious.

"It's raining," he said. "Bad day to come."

Allie and I were both wearing macks, and I carried the umbrella. He looked lengthily at these preparations and finally shrugged.

"Better come on, then."

He himself wore a raincoat and a droopy hat that had suffered downpours for years. He led the way out of the office and across the first quadrangle, with Allie and me close under my umbrella behind him.

He flicked the bolts on one of the brown doors and pulled both halves open.

"Wrecker," he said.

We went into the box. Wrecker, a leggy boy yearling colt with a nervous disposition, moved hastily away across the peat that covered the floor. Trevor Kennet made no effort to reassure him but stood foursquare looking at him with an assessing eye. Jody, for all his faults, had been good with young stock. fondling them and talking to them with affection. I thought I might have chosen badly, sending Wrecker here.

"He needs a gentle lad," I said.

Kennet's expression was open scorn. "Doesn't do to mollycoddle them. Soft horses win nothing."

End of conversation.

We went out into the rain and he slammed the bolts home. Four boxes further along, he stopped again.

"Hermes."

Again the silent appraisal. Hermes, from the experience of two full racing seasons, could look at humans without anxiety, and merely stared back. Ordinary to look at, he had won several races in masterly fashion . . . and lost every time I'd seriously backed him. Toward the end of the flat season, he had twice trailed in badly toward the rear of the field. Too much racing, Jody had said. Needed a holiday.

"What do you think of him?" I asked.

"He's eating well," Kennet said.

I waited for more, but nothing came. After a short pause, we trooped out again into the rain, and more or less repeated the whole depressing procedure in the box of my third colt, Bubbleglass.

I had great hopes for Bubbleglass. A late-developing two-year-old, he had run only once so far, and without much distinction. At three, though, he might be fun. He had grown and filled out since I'd seen him last. When I said so, Kennet remarked that it was only to be expected.

We all went back to the office. Kennet offered us coffee and looked relieved when I said we'd better be going.

"What an utterly dreary place," Allie said as we drove away.

"Designed to discourage owners from calling too often, I dare say."

She was surprised. "Do you mean it?"

"Some trainers think owners should pay their bills and shut up."

"That's crazy."

I glanced sidewise at her.

She said positively, "If I was spending all that dough, I'd sure expect to be welcomed."

"Biting the hand that feeds is a national sport."

"You're all nuts."

"How about some lunch?"

We stopped at a pub that did a fair job for a Monday, and in the afternoon we drove comfortably back to London. Allie made no objections when I pulled up outside my own front door, and followed me in through it with none of the prickly reservations I'd feared.

I lived in the two lower floors of a narrow house in Prince Albert Road overlooking Regents' Park. At street level: garage, cloakroom, workshop. Upstairs: bed, bath, kitchen, and sitting room, the last with a balcony half as big as itself. I switched on lights and led the way.

"A bachelor's pad if ever I saw one," Allie said, looking around her. "Not a frill in sight." She walked across and looked out through the sliding glass wall to the balcony. "Don't you just hate all that traffic?"

Cars drove incessantly along the road below, yellow sidelights shining through the glistening rain.

"I quite like it," I said. "In the summer, I practically live out there on the balcony, breathing in great lung-fuls of exhaust fumes and waiting for the clouds to roll away."

She laughed, unbuttoned her mack, and took it off. The red dress underneath looked as unwrinkled as it had at lunch. She was the one splash of bright color in that room of creams and browns, and she was femi-nine enough to know it.

"Drink?" I suggested.

"It's a bit early." She looked around her as if she had expected to see more than sofas and chairs. "Don't you keep any of your toys here?"

"In the workshop," I said. "Downstairs."

"I'd love to see them."

"All right."

We went down to the hall again and turned toward the back of the house. I opened the civilized wood-paneled door that led straight from carpet to concrete, from white collar to blue, from champagne to tea breaks. The familiar smell of oil and machinery waited there in the dark. I switched on the stark bright lights and stood aside for her to go through.

"But it *is* . . . a factory." She sounded astonished.

"What did you expect?"

"Oh, I don't know. Something much smaller, I guess."

The workshop was forty feet long and was the reason I had bought the house on my twenty-third birthday with money I had earned myself. Selling off the three top floors had given me enough back to construct my own first-floor flat, but the heart of the matter lay here, legacy of an old-fashioned light engineering firm that had gone bust.

The pulley system that drove nearly the whole works from one engine was the original, even if it was now powered by electricity instead of steam, and although I had replaced one or two and added another, the old machines still worked well.

"Explain it to me," Allie said.

"Well, this electric engine here"—I showed her its compact floor-mounted shape—"drives that endless belt, which goes up there round that big wheel."

"Yes." She looked up where I pointed.

"The wheel is fixed to that long shaft, which stretches right down the workshop, near the ceiling. When it rotates, it drives all those other endless belts going down to the machines. Look, I'll show you."

I switched on the electric motor and immediately the big belt from it turned the wheel, which rotated the shaft, which set the other belts circling from the shaft down to the machines. The only noises were the hum of the engines, the gentle whine of the spinning shaft, and the soft slapping of the belts.

"It looks alive," Allie said. "How do you make the machines work?"

"Engage a sort of gear inside the belt, then the belt revolves the spindle of the machine."

"Like a sewing machine," Allie said.

"More or less."

We walked down the row. She wanted to know what job each did, and I told her.

"That's a milling machine, for flat surfaces. That's a speed lathe; I use that for wood as well as metal. That tiny lathe came from a watchmaker for ultra-fine work.

That's a press. That's a polisher. That's a hacksaw. And that's a drilling machine; it bores holes downwards."

I turned round and pointed to the other side of the workshop.

"That big one on its own is an engine lathe, for heavier jobs. It has its own electric power."

"It's incredible. All this."

"Just for toys?"

"Well . . ."

"Those machines are all basically simple. They just save a lot of time."

"Do toys have to be so—well, *accurate?*"

"I mostly make the prototypes in metal and wood. Quite often they reach the shops in plastic, but unless the engineering's right in the first place the toys don't work very well, and break easily."

"Where do you keep them?" She looked around at the bare well-swept area with no work in sight.

"Over there. In the right-hand cupboard."

I went over with her and opened the big double doors. She pulled them wider with outstretched arms.

"Oh!" She looked utterly astounded.

She stood in front of the shelves with her mouth open and her eyes staring, just like a child.

"Oh," she said again, as if she could get no breath to say anything else. "Oh . . . they're the Rola toys!"

"Yes, that's right."

"Why didn't you say so?"

"Habit, really. I never do."

She gave me a smile without turning her eyes away from the bright-colored rows in the cupboard. "Do so many people ask for free samples?"

"It's just that I get tired of talking about them."

"But I played with them myself." She switched her gaze abruptly in my direction, looking puzzled. "I had a lot of them in the States ten or twelve years ago." Her voice plainly implied that I was too young to have made those.

"I was only fifteen when I did the first one," I

explained. "I had an uncle who had a workshop in the garage. He was a welder, himself. He'd shown me how to use tools from the time I was six. He was pretty shrewd. He made me take out patents before I showed my idea to anyone, and he raised and lent me the money to pay for them."

"Pay?"

"Patents are expensive, and you have to take out one for each different country, if you don't want your idea pinched. Japan, I may say, costs the most."

"Good heavens." She turned back to the cupboard, put out her hand, and lifted out the foundation of all my fortunes, the merry-go-round.

"I had the carrousel," she said. "Just like this, but different colors." She twirled the center spindle between finger and thumb so that the platform revolved and the little horses rose and fell on their poles. "I simply can't believe it."

She put the merry-go-round back in its slot and one by one lifted out several of the others, exclaiming over old friends and investigating the strangers. "Do you have a Rola base down here?"

"Sure," I said, lifting it from the bottom of the cupboard.

"Oh, do let me—please?" She was as excited as if she were still a little girl. I carried the base over to the workbench and laid it there, and she came over with four of the toys.

The Rola base consisted of a large flat box, in this case two feet square by six inches deep, though several other sizes had been made. From one side protruded a handle for winding, and one had to have that side of the Rola base aligned with the edge of the table, so that winding was possible. Inside the box were the rollers that gave the toy its phonetic Rola name: wide rollers carrying a long flat continuous belt inset with many rows of sidewise-facing cogwheel teeth. In the top of the box were corresponding rows of holes: dozens of holes altogether. Each of the separate mechanical toys, like the merry-go-round and a hun-

dred others, had a central spindle that protruded down
from beneath the toy and was grooved like a cogwheel.
When one slipped any spindle through any hole, it
engaged on the belt of cog teeth below, and when one
turned the single handle in the Rola base, the wide belt
of cog teeth moved endlessly round and all the spindles
rotated and all the toys performed their separate tasks.
A simple locking device on the base of each toy engaged with stops by each hole to prevent the toy rotat-
ing as a whole.

Allie had brought the carrousel and the roller coaster
from the fairground set, and a cow from the farm set,
and the firing tank from the army set. She slotted the
spindles through random holes and turned the handle.
The merry-go-round went round and round, the trucks
went up and down the roller coaster, the cow nodded its
head and swished its tail, and the tank rotated with
sparks coming out of its gun barrel.

She laughed with pleasure.

"I don't believe it. I simply don't believe it. I never
dreamed you could have made the Rola toys."

"I've made others, though."

"What sort?"

"Um . . . the latest in the shops is a coding machine.
It's doing quite well this Christmas."

"You don't mean the Secret Coder?"

"Yes." I was surprised she knew of it.

"Do show me. My sister's giving one each to the
boys, but they were already gift-wrapped."

So I showed her the coder, which looked like provid-
ing me with race horses for some time to come, as a lot
of people besides children had found it compulsive.
The new adult version was much more complicated but
also much more expensive, which somewhat increased
the royalties.

From the outside, the children's version looked like a
box, smaller than a shoe box, with a sloping top surface. Set in this were letter keys exactly like a conventional typewriter, except that there were no numbers,
no punctuation marks, and no space bar.

"How does it work?" Allie asked.

"You type your message, and it comes out in code."

"Just like that?"

"Try it."

She gave me an amused look, turned so that I couldn't see her fingers, and with one hand expertly typed about twenty-five letters. From the end of the box a narrow paper strip emerged, with letters typed on it in groups of five.

"What now?"

"Tear the strip off," I said.

She did that. "It's like ticker tape," she said.

"It is. Same size, anyway."

She held it out to me. I looked at it and came as close to blushing as I'm ever likely to.

"Can you read it just like that?" she exclaimed. "Some coder, if you can read it at a glance."

"I invented the damn thing," I said. "I know it by heart."

"How does it work?"

"There's a cylinder inside with twelve complete alphabets on it, each arranged in a totally random manner, and all different. You set this dial here, see"—I showed her—"to any numbers from one to twelve. Then you type your message. Inside, the keys don't print the letter you press on the outside, but the letter that's aligned with it inside. There's an automatic spring which jumps after every five presses, so the message comes out in groups of five."

"It's fantastic. . . . My sister says the boys have been asking for them for weeks. Lots of children they know have them, all sending weird secret messages all over the place and driving their mothers wild."

"You can make more involved codes by feeding the coded message through again, or backwards," I said. "Or by switching the code number every few letters. All the child receiving the message needs to know is the numbers he has to set on his own dial."

"How do I decode this?"

"Put that tiny lever—there—down instead of up, and just type the coded message. It will come out as it went in . . . except still in groups of five letters, of course. Try it."

She looked confused. She screwed up the tape and laughed, "I guess I don't need to."

"Would you like one?" I asked diffidently.

"I certainly would."

"Blue or red?"

"Red."

In another cupboard, I had a pile of manufactured coders packed like those in the shops. I opened one of the cartons, checked that the contents had a bright-red plastic casing, and handed it over.

"If you write me a Christmas message," she said, "I'll expect it in Code Number Four."

I took her out to dinner again, as I was on a bacon-and-egg level myself as a cook, and she was, after all, on holiday to get away from the kitchen.

There was nothing new in taking a girl to dinner. Nothing exceptional, I supposed, in Allie herself. I liked her directness, her naturalness. She was supremely easy to be with, not interpreting occasional silences as personal insults, not coy or demanding, nor sexually a tease. Not, either, a girl of hungry intellect, but certainly of good sense.

That wasn't all, of course. The spark that attracts one person to another was there, too, and on her side also, I thought.

I drove her back to Hampstead and stopped outside her sister's house.

"Tomorrow?" I said.

She didn't answer directly. "I go home on Thursday."

"I know. What time is your flight?"

"Not till the evening. Six-thirty."

"Can I drive you to the airport?"

"I could get my sister . . ."

"I'd like to."

"Okay."

We sat in a short silence.

"Tomorrow," she said finally. "I guess . . . if you like."

"Yes."

She nodded briefly, opened the car door, and spoke over her shoulder. "Thank you for a fascinating day."

She was out on the pavement before I got round to help her. She smiled as I approached. Purring and contented, as far as I could judge.

"Good night." She held out her hand.

I took it, and at the same time leaned down and kissed her cheek. We looked at each other, her hand still in mine. One simply cannot waste such opportunities. I repeated the kiss, but on her lips.

She kissed as I'd expected, with friendliness and reservations. I kissed her twice more on the same terms.

"Good night," she said again, smiling.

I watched her wave before she shut her sister's front door, and drove home wishing she were still with me. When I got back, I went into the workshop and retrieved the screwed-up piece of code she'd thrown in the litter bin. Smoothing it, I read the jumbled-up letters again.

No mistake. Sorted out, the words were still a pat on the ego.

"The toyman is as great as his toys."

I put the scrap of paper in my wallet and went upstairs to bed feeling the world's biggest fool.

5

On Wednesday morning, Charlie Canterfield telephoned at seven-thirty. I stretched a hand sleepily out of bed and groped for the receiver.

"Hullo?"

"Where the hell have you been?" Charlie said. "I've been trying your number since Sunday morning."

"Out."

"I know that." He sounded more amused than irritated. "Look . . . can you spare me some time today?"

"All of it, if you like."

My generosity was solely due to the unfortunate fact that Allie had felt bound to spend her last full day with her sister, who had bought tickets and made plans. I had gathered that she'd only given me Monday and Tuesday at the expense of her other commitments, so I couldn't grumble. Tuesday had been even better than Monday, except for ending in exactly the same way.

"This morning will do," Charlie said. "Nine-thirty?"

"Okay. Amble along."

"I want to bring a friend."

"Fine. Do you know how to get here?"

"A taxi will find it," Charlie said, and disconnected.

Charlie's friend turned out to be a large man of

Charlie's age with shoulders like a docker and language to match.

"Bert Huggerneck," Charlie said, making introductions.

Bert Huggerneck crunched my bones in his muscular hand. "Any friend of Charlie's is a friend of mine," he said, but with no warmth or conviction.

"Come upstairs," I said. "Coffee? Or breakfast?"

"Coffee," Charlie said. Bert Huggerneck said he didn't mind, which proved in the end to be bacon and tomato ketchup on toast twice, with curried baked beans on the side. He chose the meal himself from my meager storage cupboard, and ate with speed and enjoyment.

"Not a bad bit of bleeding nosh," he observed. "Considering."

"Considering what?" I asked.

He gave me a sharp look over a well-filled fork, and made a gesture embracing both the flat and its neighborhood. "Considering you must be a rich bleeding capitalist, living here." He pronounced it "ca*pit*alist," and clearly considered it one of the worst of insults.

"Come off it," Charlie said amiably. "His breeding's as impeccable as yours and mine."

"Huh." Total disbelief didn't stop Bert Huggerneck accepting more toast. "Got any jam?" he said.

"Sorry."

He made do with half a jar of marmalade.

"What's that about breeding?" he said suspiciously to Charlie. "Ca*pit*alists are all snobs."

"His grandfather was a mechanic," Charlie said. "Same as mine was a milkman and yours a navvy."

I was amused that Charlie had glossed over my father and mother, who had been schoolteacher and nurse. Far more respectable to be able to refer to the grandfather-mechanic, the welder-uncle, and the host of card-carrying cousins. If politicians of all sorts searched diligently amongst their antecedents for proletarianism and denied aristocratic contacts three times before cockcrow every weekday morning, who was I to spoil the fun? In truth, the two seemingly divergent lines of manual work and schoolmastering had given me the best of both worlds, the ability to use my hands and the education to design things for them to make. Money and experience had done the rest.

"I gather Mr. Huggerneck is here against his will," I observed.

"Don't you believe it," Charlie said. "He wants your help."

"How does he act if he wants to kick you in the kidneys?"

"He wouldn't eat your food."

Fair enough, I thought. Accept a man's salt, and you didn't boot him. Times hadn't collapsed altogether where that still held good.

We were sitting round the kitchen table, with Charlie smoking a cigarette and using his saucer as an ashtray and me wondering what he considered so urgent. Bert wiped his plate with a spare piece of toast and washed it down with coffee.

"What's for lunch?" he said.

I took it as it was meant, as thanks for breakfast.

"Bert," said Charlie, coming to the point, "is a book-ie's clerk."

"Hold on," Bert said. "Not is. Was."

"Was," Charlie conceded. "And will be again. But at the moment the firm he worked for is bankrupt."

"The boss went spare," Bert said, nodding. "The bums come and took away all the bleeding office desks and that."

"And all the bleeding typists?"

"Here," said Bert, his brows suddenly lifting as a smile forced itself at least into his eyes. "You're not all bad, then."

"Rotten to the core," I said. "Go on."

"Well, see, the boss got all his bleeding sums wrong, or, like he said, his mathematical computations were based on a misconception."

"Like the wrong horse won?"

Bert's smile got nearer. "Cotton on quick, don't you? A whole bleeding row of wrong horses. Here, see, I've been writing for him for bleeding years. All the big courses, he has—well, he had—a stand in Tatt's and down in the Silver Ring, too, and I've been writing for him myself most of the time. For him personally, see?"

"Yes." Bookmakers always took a clerk to record all bets as they were made. A bookmaking firm of any size sent out a team of two men or more to every allowed enclosure at most race meetings in their area, the bigger the firm, the more meetings they covered.

"Well, see, I warned him once or twice there was a leery look to his book. See, after bleeding years you get a nose for trouble, don't you? This last year or so, he's made a right bleeding balls-up more than once and I told him he'd have the bums in if he went on like that, and I was right, wasn't I?"

"What did he say?"

"Told me to mind my own bleeding business," Bert said. "But it was my bleeding business, wasn't it? I mean, it was my job at stake. My livelihood, same as his. Who's going to pay my H.P. and rent and a few pints with the lads, I asked him, and he turned round and said not to worry, he had it all in hand, he knew what he was doing." His voice held total disgust.

"And he didn't," I remarked.

"Of course he bleeding didn't. He didn't take a blind bit of notice of what I said. Bleeding stupid, he was. Then ten days ago he really blew it. Lost a packet. The whole works. All of us got the push. No redundancy, either. He's got a bleeding big overdraft in the bank and he's up to the eyeballs in debt."

I glanced at Charlie, who seemed exclusively interested in the ash on his cigarette.

"Why," I asked Bert, "did your boss ignore your warnings and rush headlong over the cliff?"

"He didn't jump over no cliff. He's getting drunk every night down the boozer."

"I meant . . ."

"Hang on, I get you. Why did he lose the whole bleeding works? Because someone fed him the duff gen, that's my opinion. Cocky as all getout, he was, on the way to the races. Then, coming home, he tells me the firm is all washed up and down the bleeding drain. White as chalk, he was. Trembling, sort of. So I told him I'd warned him over and over. And that day I'd warned him, too, that he was laying too much on that Energise and not covering himself, and he'd told me all jolly like to mind my own effing business. So I reckon someone had told him Energise was fixed not to win, but it bleeding did win, and that's what's done for the firm."

Bert shut his mouth and the silence was as loud as bells. Charlie tapped the ash off and smiled.

I swallowed.

"Er . . ." I said eventually.

"That's only half of it," Charlie said, interrupting smoothly. "Go on, Bert, tell him the rest."

Bert seemed happy to oblige. "Well, see, there I was in the boozer Saturday evening. Last Saturday, not the day Energise won. Four days ago, see? After the bums had been, and all that. Well, in walks Charlie, like he sometimes does, and we had a couple of jars together, him and me being old mates, really, on account of we lived next door to each other when we were kids and he was going to that la-di-da bleeding Eton and someone had to take him down a peg or two in the holidays. . . . So, anyway, there we were in the boozer and I pour out all my troubles and Charlie says he has another friend who'd like to hear them, so—well, here we are."

"What are the other troubles, then?" I asked.

"Oh . . . Yeah. Well, see, the boss had a couple of betting shops. Nothing fancy, just a couple of betting shops in Windsor and Staines, see. The office, now, where the bailiffs came and took everything—that was behind the shop in Staines. So there's the boss holding his head and wailing like a siren because all his bleeding furniture's on its way out, when the phone rings. 'Course by this time the phone's down on the floor, because the desk it was on is out on the pavement. So the boss squats down beside it and there's some geezer on the other end offering to buy the lease."

He paused more for dramatic effect than breath.

"Go on," I said encouragingly.

"Manna from heaven for the boss, that was," said Bert. "See, he'd have had to go on paying the rent for both places even if they were shut. He practically fell on the neck of this geezer in a manner of speaking, and the geezer came round and paid him in cash on the nail, three hundred smackers, that very morning, and the boss has been getting drunk on it ever since."

A pause. "What line of business is this geezer in?" I asked.

"Eh?" said Bert surprised. "Bookmaking, of course."

Charlie smiled.

"I expect you've heard of him," Bert said. "Name of Ganser Mays."

It was inevitable, I supposed.

"In what way," I asked, "do you want me to help?"

"Huh?"

"Charlie said you wanted my help."

"Oh, that. I dunno, really. Charlie just said it might help to tell you what I'd told him, so I done it."

"Did Charlie tell you who owns Energise?" I asked.

"No, Charlie didn't," Charlie said.

"What the bleeding hell does it matter who owns it?" Bert demanded.

"I do," I said.

Bert looked from one of us to the other several times. Various thoughts took their turn behind his eyes, and Charlie and I waited.

"Here," he said at last. "Did you bleeding fix that race?"

"The horse ran fair and square, and I backed it on the Tote," I said.

"Well, how come my boss thought . . ."

"I've no idea," I said untruthfully.

Charlie lit another cigarette from the stub of the last. They were his lungs, after all.

"The point is," I said, "who gave your boss the wrong information?"

"Dunno." He thought it over, but shook his head. "Dunno."

"Could it have been Ganser Mays?"

"Blimey!"

"Talk about slander," Charlie said. "He'd have you for that."

"I merely ask," I said. "I also ask whether Bert knows of any other small firms which have gone out of business in the same way."

"Blimey," Bert said again, with even more force.

Charlie sighed with resignation, as if he hadn't engineered the whole morning's chat.

"Ganser Mays," I said conversationally, "has opened a vast string of betting shops during the past year or so. What has happened to the opposition?"

"Down the boozer getting drunk," Charlie said.

Charlie stayed for a while after Bert had gone, sitting more comfortably in one of my leather armchairs and reverting thankfully to his more natural self.

"Bert's a great fellow," he said. "But I find him tiring." His Eton accent, I noticed, had come back in force, and I realized with mild surprise how much he tailored his voice and manner to suit his company. The Charlie Canterfield I knew, the powerful banker smoking a cigar who thought of a million as everyday currency, was not the face he had shown to Bert Huggerneck. It occurred to me that of all the people I had met who had moved from one world to another, Charlie had done it with most success. He swam through big business like a fish in water, but he could still feel completely at home with Bert in a way that I, who had made a less radical journey, could not.

"Which is the villain," Charlie asked, "Ganser Mays or Jody Leeds?"

"Both."

"Equal partners?"

We considered it. "No way of knowing at the moment," I said.

"At the moment?" His eyebrows went up.

I smiled slightly. "I thought I might have a small crack at . . . would you call it justice?"

"The law's a bad thing to take into your own hands."

"I don't exactly aim to lynch anyone."

"What, then?"

I hesitated. "There's something I ought to check. I think I'll do it today. After that, if I'm right, I'll make a loud fuss."

"Slander actions notwithstanding?"

"I don't know." I shook my head. "It's infuriating."

"What are you going to check?" he asked.

"Telephone tomorrow morning, and I'll tell you."

Charlie, like Allie, asked before he left if I would show him where I made the toys. We went down to the workshop and found Owen Idris, my general helper, busy sweeping the tidy floor.

"Morning, Owen."

"Morning, sir."

"This is Mr. Canterfield, Owen."

"Morning, sir."

Owen appeared to have swept without pause, but I knew the swift glance he had given Charlie was as good as a photograph. My neat dry little Welsh factotum had a phenomenal memory for faces.

"Will you want the car today, sir?" he said.

"This evening."

"I'll just change the oil, then."

"Fine."

"Will you be wanting me for the parking?"

I shook my head. "Not tonight."

"Very good, sir." He looked resigned. "Any time," he said.

I showed Charlie the machines, but he knew less about engineering than I did about banking.

"Where do you start, in the hands or in the head?"

"Head," I said. "Then hands, then head."

"So clear."

"I think of something, I make it, I draw it."

"Draw it?"

"Machine drawings, not an artistic impression."

"Blueprints," said Charlie, nodding wisely.

"Blueprints are copies. . . . The originals are black on white."

"Disillusioning."

I slid open one of the long drawers that held the designs and showed him some of them. The fine spidery lines with a key giving details of materials and signs of screw threads were very different from the bright shiny toys that reached the shops, and Charlie looked from design to finished article slowly shaking his head.

"Don't know how you do it."

"Training," I said. "Same way that you switch money round ten currencies in half an hour and end up thousands richer."

"Can't do that so much these days," he said gloomily. He watched me put designs and toys away. "Don't forget, though, that my firm can always find finances for good ideas."

"I won't forget."

"There must be a dozen merchant banks," Charlie said, "all hoping to be nearest when you look around for cash."

"The manufacturers fix the cash. I just collect the royalties."

He shook his head. "You'll never make a million that way."

"I won't get ulcers, either."

"No ambition?"

"To win the Derby and get even with Jody
Leeds."

I arrived at Jody's expensive stable uninvited, quietly, at half past midnight, and on foot. The car lay
parked half a mile behind me, along with prudence.

Pale fitful moonlight lit glimpses of the large manor
house with its pedimented front door and rows of uniform windows. No lights shone upstairs in the room
Jody shared with Felicity, and none downstairs in the
large drawing room beneath. The lawn, rough now and
scattered with a few last dead leaves, stretched peace-
fully from the house to where I stood hidden in the
bushes by the gate.

I watched for a while. There was no sign of anyone
awake or moving, and I hadn't expected it. Jody, like
most six-thirty risers, was usually asleep by eleven at
the latest, and telephone calls after ten were answered
brusquely if at all. On the other hand, he had no
reservations about telephoning others in the morning
before seven. He had no patience with life patterns
unlike his own.

To the right and slightly to the rear of the house
were the dimly gleaming roofs of the stables. White-
railed paddocks lay around and beyond them, with big
plane trees growing at landscaped corners. When
Berksdown Court had been built, cost had come second
to excellence.

Carrying a large black rubber-clad torch, unlit, I
walked softly up the drive and round toward the
horses. No dogs barked. No all-night guards sprang out
to ask my business. Silence and peace bathed the whole
place undisturbed.

My breath, all the same, came faster. My heart
thumped. It would be bad if anyone caught me. I had
tried reassuring myself that Jody would do me no
actual physical harm, but I hadn't found myself convinced. Anger, as when I'd stood in the path of the
horse box, was again thrusting me into risk.

Close to the boxes, one could hear little more than

from a distance. Jody's horses stood on sawdust now that straw prices had trebled, and made no rustle when they moved though a sudden equine sneeze made me jump.

Jody's yard was not a regular quadrangle but a series of three-sided courts of unequal size and powerful charm. There were forty boxes altogether, few enough in any case to support such a lavish establishment, but since my horses had left I guessed there were only about twenty inmates remaining. Jody was in urgent need of another mug.

He had always economized on labor, reckoning that he and Felicity between them could do the work of four. His inexhaustible energy in fact insured that no lads stayed in the yard very long, as they couldn't stand the pace. Since the last so-called head lad had left in dudgeon because Jody constantly usurped his authority, there had been no one but Jody himself in charge. It was unlikely, I thought, that in the present circumstances he would have taken on another man, which meant that the cottage at the end of the yard would be empty.

There were, at any rate, no lights in it, and no anxious figure came scurrying out to see about the stranger in the night. I went with care to the first box in the first court and quietly slid back the bolts.

Inside stood a large chestnut mare languidly eating hay. She turned her face unexcitedly in the torchlight. A big white blaze down her forehead and nose. Asphodel.

I shut her door, inching home the bolts. Any unusual sharp noise would carry clearly through the cold calm air, and Jody's subconscious ears would never sleep. The second box contained a heavy bay gelding with black points, the third a dark chestnut with one white sock. I went slowly round the first section of stables, shining the torch at each horse.

Instead of settling, my nerves got progressively worse. I had not yet found what I'd come for, and every passing minute made discovery more possible. I was careful with the torch. Careful with the bolts. My breath was shallow. I decided I'd make a rotten burglar.

Box No. 10, in the next section, contained a dark-brown gelding with no markings. The next box housed an undistinguished bay, the next another, and the next another. After that came an almost black horse with a slightly Arab-looking nose, another very dark horse, and two more bays. The next three boxes all contained chestnuts, all unremarkable to my eyes. The last inhabited box held the only gray.

I gently shut the door of the gray and returned to the box of the chestnut next door. Went inside. Shone my torch over him carefully inch by inch.

I came to no special conclusion except that I didn't know enough about horses.

I'd done all I could. Time to go home. Time for my heart to stop thudding at twice the speed of sound. I turned for the door.

Lights came on in a blaze. Startled, I took one step toward the door. Only one.

Three men crowded into the opening.

Jody Leeds.

Ganser Mays.

Another man, whom I didn't know, whose appearance scarcely inspired joy and confidence. He was large, hard, and muscular, and he wore thick leather gloves, a cloth cap pulled forward, and, at one-thirty in the morning, sunglasses.

Whomever they had expected, it wasn't me. Jody's face held a mixture of consternation and anger, with the former winning by a mile.

"What the bloody hell are you doing here?" he said.

There was no possible answer.

"He isn't leaving," Ganser Mays said. The eyes behind the metal rims were narrowed with ill intent and the long nose protruded sharply like a dagger. The urbane manner that lulled the clients while he relieved them of their cash had turned into the naked viciousness of the threatened criminal. Too late to worry that I'd cast myself in the role of threat.

"What?" Jody turned his face to him, not understanding.

"He isn't leaving."

Jody said, "How are you going to stop him?"

Nobody told him. Nobody told me, either. I took two steps toward the exit and found out.

The large man said nothing at all, but it was he who moved. A large gloved fist crashed into my ribs at the business end of a highly efficient short jab. Breath left my lungs faster than nature intended, and I had difficulty getting it back.

Beyond schoolboy scuffles, I had never seriously had to defend myself. No time to learn. I slammed an elbow at Jody's face, kicked Ganser Mays in the stomach, and tried for the door.

Muscles in cap and sunglasses knew all that I didn't. An inch or two taller, a stone or two heavier, and warmed to his task. I landed one respectable punch on the junction of his nose and mouth in return for a couple of bangs over the heart, and made no progress toward freedom.

Jody and Ganser Mays recovered from my first onslaught and clung to me like limpets, one on each arm. I staggered under their combined weight. Muscles measured his distance and flung his bunched hand at my jaw. I managed to move my head just in time, and felt the leather glove burn my cheek. Then the other fist came round, faster and crossing, and hit me square. I fell reeling across the box, released suddenly by Ganser Mays and Jody, and my head smashed solidly into the iron bars of the manger.

Total instant unconsciousness was the result.

Death must be like that, I suppose.

6

Life came back in an incomprehensible blur.

I couldn't see properly. Couldn't focus. Heard strange noises. Couldn't control my body, couldn't move my legs, couldn't lift my head. Tongue paralyzed. Brain whirling. Everything disconnected and hazy.

"Drunk," someone said distinctly.

The word made no sense. It wasn't I who was drunk.

"Paralytic."

The ground was wet. Shining. Dazzled my eyes. I was sitting on it. Slumped on it, leaning against something hard. I shut my eyes against the drizzle and that made the whirling worse. I could feel myself falling. Banged my head. Cheek in the wet. Nose in the wet. Lying on the hard wet ground. There was a noise like rain.

"Bloody amazing," said a voice.

"Come on, then, let's be having you."

Strong hands slid under my armpits and grasped my ankles. I couldn't struggle. Couldn't understand where I was or what was happening.

It seemed vaguely that I was in the back of a car. I could smell the upholstery. My nose was on it. Someone was breathing very loudly. Almost snoring. Someone spoke. A jumbled mixture of sounds that made no words. It couldn't have been me. Couldn't have been.

The car jerked to a sudden stop. The driver swore. I rolled off the seat and passed out.

Next thing, bright lights and people carrying me as before.

I tried to say something. It came out in a jumble. This time I knew the jumble came from my own mouth.

"Waking up again," someone said.

"Get him out of here before he's sick."

March, march. More carrying. Loud boots on echoing floors.

"He's bloody heavy."

"Bloody nuisance."

The whirling went on. The whole building was spinning like a merry-go-round.

Merry-go-round.

The first feeling of identity came back. I wasn't just a lump of weird disorientated sensations. Somewhere, deep inside, I was . . . somebody.

Merry-go-rounds swam in and out of consciousness. I found I was lying on a bed. Bright light blinded me every time I tried to open my eyes. The voices went away.

Time passed.

I began to feel exceedingly ill. Heard someone moaning. Didn't think it was me. After a while, I knew it was, which made it possible to stop.

Feet coming back. March, march. Two pairs at least.

"What's your name?"

What was my name? Couldn't remember.

"He's soaking wet."

"What do you expect? He was sitting on the pavement in the rain."

"Take his jacket off."

They took my jacket off, sitting me up to do it. I lay down again. My trousers were pulled off and someone put a blanket over me.

"He's dead drunk."

"Yes. Have to make sure, though. They're always an infernal nuisance like this. You simply can't risk that they haven't bumped their skulls and got a hairline fracture. . . . You don't want them dying on you in the night."

I tried to tell him I wasn't drunk. Hairline fracture . . . Christ . . . I didn't want to wake up dead in the morning.

"What did you say?"

I tried again. "Not drunk," I said.

Someone laughed without mirth.

"Just smell his breath."

How did I know I wasn't drunk? The answer eluded me. I just knew I wasn't drunk . . . because I knew I hadn't drunk enough . . . or any . . . alcohol. How did I know? I just knew. How did I know?

While these hopeless thoughts spiraled around in the chaos inside my head, a lot of strange fingers were feeling around in my hair.

"He *has* banged his head, damn it. There's quite a large swelling."

"He's no worse than when they brought him in, Doc. Better, if anything."

"Scott," I said suddenly.

"What's that?"

"Scott."

"Is that your name?"

I tried to sit up. The light whirled giddily.

"Where . . . am I?"

"That what they all say."

"In a cell, my lad, that's where."

In a cell.

"What?" I said.

"In a cell at Savile Row police station. Drunk and incapable."

I couldn't be.

"Look, Constable, I'll just take a blood test. Then I'll do those other jobs, then come back and look at him, to make sure. I don't think we've a fracture here, but we can't take the chance."

"Right, Doc."

The prick of a needle reached me dimly. Waste of time, I thought. Wasn't drunk. What was I . . . besides ill, giddy, lost and stuck in limbo? Didn't know. Couldn't be bothered to think. Slid without struggling into a whirling black sleep.

The next awakening was in all ways worse. For a start, I wasn't ready to be dragged back from the dark. My head ached abominably, bits of my body hurt a good deal, and over all I felt like an advanced case of seasickness.

"Wakey, wakey, rise and shine. Cup of tea for you and you don't deserve it."

I opened my eyes. The bright light was still there but now identifiable not as some gross moon but as a simple electric bulb near the ceiling.

I shifted my gaze to where the voice had come from. A middle-aged policeman stood there with a paper cup in one hand. Behind him, an open door to a corridor. All round me, the close walls of a cell. I lay on a reasonably comfortable bed with two blankets keeping me warm.

"Sobering up, are you?"

"I wasn't . . . drunk." My voice came out hoarse and my mouth felt as furry as a mink coat.

The policeman held out the cup. I struggled onto one elbow and took it from him.

"Thanks." The tea was strong, hot, and sweet. I wasn't sure it didn't make me feel even sicker.

"The doc's been back twice to check on you. You were drunk all right. Banged your head, too."

"But I wasn't . . ."

"You sure were. The doc did a blood test to make certain."

"Where are my clothes?"

"Oh, yeah. We took 'em off. They were wet. I'll get them."

He went out without shutting the door and I spent

the few minutes he was away trying to sort out what was happening. I could remember bits of the night, but hazily. I knew who I was. No problem there. I looked at my watch: seven-thirty. I felt absolutely lousy.

The policeman returned with my suit, which was wrinkled beyond belief and looked nothing like the one I'd set out in.

Set out . . . Where to?

"Is this . . . Savile Row? West end of London?"

"You remember being brought in, then?"

"Some of it. Not much."

"The patrol car picked you up somewhere in Soho at around four o'clock this morning."

"What was I doing there?"

"I don't know, do I? Nothing, as far as I know. Just sitting dead drunk on the pavement in the pouring rain."

"Why did they bring me here if I wasn't doing anything?"

"To save you from yourself," he said without rancor. "Drunks make more trouble if we leave them than if we bring them in, so we bring them in. Can't have drunks wandering out into the middle of the road and causing accidents or breaking their silly skulls falling over or waking up violent and smashing shopwindows as some of them do."

"I feel ill."

"What d'you expect? If you're going to be sick, there's a bucket at the end of the bed."

He gave me a nod in which sympathy wasn't entirely lacking, and took himself away.

About an hour later, I was driven with three other gentlemen in the same plight to attend the Malborough Street Magistrates' Court. Drunks, it seemed, were first on the agenda. Every day's agenda.

In the interim, I had become reluctantly convinced of three things.

First was that even though I could not remember drinking, I had at 4 A.M. that morning been hopelessly intoxicated. The blood test, analyzed at speed because of the bang on my head, had revealed a level of 290 milligrams of alcohol per centiliter of blood, which, I had been assured, meant that I had drunk the equivalent of at least half a bottle of spirits during the preceding few hours.

The second was that it would make no difference at all if I could convince anyone that at one-thirty I had been stone cold sober seventy miles away in Berkshire. They would merely say I had plenty of time to get drunk on the journey.

And the third and perhaps least welcome of all was that I seemed to have collected far more sore spots than I could account for.

I had remembered, bit by bit, my visit to Jody. I remembered trying to fight all three men at once, which was an idiotic sort of thing to attempt in the first place, even without the casual expertise of the man in the sunglasses. I remembered the squashy feel when my fist connected with his nose, and I knew all about the punches he'd given me in return. Even so . . .

I shrugged. Perhaps I didn't remember it all, as I didn't remember getting drunk. Or perhaps . . . Well, Ganser Mays and Jody both had reason to dislike me, and Jody had been wearing jodhpur boots.

The court proceedings took ten minutes. The charge was "drunk in charge." In charge of what, I asked. In charge of the police, they said.

"Guilty or not guilty?"

"Guilty," I said resignedly.

"Fined five pounds. Do you need time to pay?"

"No, sir."

"Good. Next, please."

Outside, in the little office where I was due to pay the fine, I telephoned Owen Idris. Paying, after all, had been a problem, as there had proved to be no wallet in my rough-dried suit. No checkbook, either—nor, when I came to think of it, any keys. Were they all by any chance at Savile Row, I asked. Someone telephoned. No, they weren't. I had had nothing at all in my pockets when I was picked up. No means of identification, no money, no keys, no pen, no handkerchief.

"Owen? Bring ten pounds and a taxi to Marlborough Street Court."

"Very good, sir."

"Right away."

"Of course."

I felt hopelessly groggy. I sat in an upright chair to wait, and wondered how long it took for half a bottle of spirits to dry out.

Owen came in thirty minutes and handed me the money without comment. Even his face showed no surprise at finding me in such a predicament, and unshaven into the bargain. I wasn't sure that I appreciated his lack of surprise. I also couldn't think of any believable explanation. Nothing to do but shrug it off, pay the five pounds, and get home as best I could. Owen sat beside me in the taxi and gave me small sidelong glances every hundred yards or so.

I made it upstairs to the sitting room and lay down flat on the sofa. Owen had stayed behind to pay the taxi and I could hear him talking to someone down in the hall. I could do without visitors, I thought. I could do without everything except twenty-four hours of oblivion.

The visitor was Charlie.

"Your man says you're in trouble."

"Mmm."

"Good God." He was standing beside me, looking down. "What on earth have you been doing?"

"Long story."

"Hmm . . . Will your man get us some coffee?"

"Ask him. . . . He'll be in the workshop. Intercom over there." I nodded toward the far door and wished I hadn't. My whole brain felt like a bruise.

Charlie talked to Owen on the intercom, and Owen came up with his ultra-polite face and messed around with filters in the kitchen.

"What's the matter with you?" Charlie asked.

"Knocked out, drunk, and—" I stopped.

"And what?"

"Nothing."

"You need a doctor."

"I saw a police surgeon. Or, rather, he saw me."

"You can't see the state of your eyes," Charlie said seriously. "And whether you like it or not, I'm getting you a doctor." He went away to the kitchen to consult Owen, and I heard the extension bell there tinkling as he kept his promise. He came back.

"What's wrong with my eyes?"

"Pinpoint pupils and glassy daze."

"Charming."

Owen brought the coffee, which smelled fine, but I found I could scarcely drink it. Both men looked at me with what I could only call concern.

"How did you get like this?" Charlie asked.

"Shall I go, sir?" Owen said politely.

"No. Sit down, Owen. You may as well know, too." He sat comfortably in a small armchair, neither perching on the front nor lolling at ease in the depths. The compromise of Owen's attitude to me was what made him above price, his calm understanding that although I paid for work done, we each retained equal dignity in the transaction. I had employed him for less than a year, I hoped he would stay till he dropped.

"I went down to Jody Leeds's stable last night, after dark," I said. "I had no right at all to be there. Jody and two other men found me in one of the boxes looking at a horse. There was a bit of a struggle, and I banged my head—on the manger, I think—and got knocked out."

I stopped for breath. My audience said nothing at all.

"When I woke up, I was sitting on a pavement in Soho, dead drunk."

"Impossible," Charlie said.

"No. It happened. The police scooped me up, as they apparently do to all drunks littering the footpaths. I spent the remains of the night in a cell and got fined five pounds, and here I am."

There was a long pause.

Charlie cleared his throat. "Er . . . various questions arise."

"They do indeed."

Owen said calmly, "The car, sir. Where did you leave the car?" The car was his special love, polished and cared for like silver.

I told him exactly where I'd parked it. Also that I no longer had its keys. Nor the keys to the flat or the workshop, for that matter.

Both Charlie and Owen showed alarm and agreed between themselves that the first thing Owen would do, even before fetching the car, would be to change all my locks.

"I made those locks," I protested.

"Do you want Jody walking in here while you're asleep?"

"No."

"Then Owen changes the locks."

I didn't demur any more. I'd been thinking of a new form of lock for some time, but hadn't actually made it. I would soon. though. . . . I would patent it and make it as a toy for kids to lock up their secrets, and maybe in twenty years' time half the doors in the country would be keeping our burglars that way. My lock didn't need keys or electronics, and couldn't be picked. It stood there, clear and sharp in my mind, with all its working parts meshing neatly.

"Are you all right?" Charlie said abruptly.

"What?"

"For a moment you looked—" He stopped and didn't finish the sentence.

"I'm not dying. if that's what you think. It's just that . . . I've an idea for a new sort of lock."

Charlie's attention sharpened as quickly as it had at Sandown.

"Revolutionary?" he asked hopefully.

I smiled inside. The word was apt in more ways than one, as some of the lock's works would revolve.

"You might say so," I said.

"Don't forget . . . my bank."

"I won't."

"No one but you would be inventing things when he's half dead."

"I may look half dead," I said, "but I'm not." I might feel half dead, too, I thought, but it would all pass.

The doorbell rang sharply.

"If it's anyone but the doctor," Charlie told Owen, "tell them our friend is out."

Owen nodded briefly and went downstairs, but when he came back he brought not the doctor but a visitor less expected and more welcome.

"Miss Ward, sir."

She was through the door before he had the words out, blowing in like a gust of fresh air, her face as smooth and clean and her clothes as well groomed as mine were dirty and squalid. She looked like life itself on two legs, her vitality lighting the room.

"Steven!"

She stopped dead a few feet from the sofa, staring down. She glanced at Charlie and at Owen. "What's the matter with him?"

"Rough night on the tiles," I said. "D'you mind if I don't get up?"

"How do you do?" Charlie said politely. "I am Charlie Canterfield. Friend of Steven's." He shook hands with her.

"Alexandra Ward," she replied, looking bemused.

"You've met," I said.

"What?"

"In Walton Street."

They looked at each other and realized what I meant. Charlie began to tell Allie how I had arrived in this sorry state, and Owen went out shopping for locks. I lay on the sofa and drifted. The whole morning seemed disjointed and jerky to me, as if my thought processes were tripping over cracks.

Allie pulled up a squashy leather stool and sat beside me, which brought recovery nearer. She put her hand on mine. Better still.

"You're crazy," she said.

I sighed. Couldn't have everything.

"Have you forgotten I'm going home this evening?"

"I have not," I said. "Though it looks now as though I'll have to withdraw my offer of driving you to the airport. I don't think I'm fit. No car, for another thing."

"That's actually what I came for." She hesitated. "I have to keep peace with my sister—" She stopped, leaving a world of family tensions hovering unspoken. "I came to say goodbye."

"What sort of goodbye?"

"What do you mean?"

"Goodbye for now," I said, "or goodbye forever?"

"Which would you like?"

Charlie chuckled. "Now there's a double-edged question if I ever heard one."

"You're not supposed to be listening," she said with mock severity.

"Goodbye for now," I said.

"All right." She smiled the flashing smile. "Suits me."

Charlie wandered round the room looking at things but showed no signs of going. Allie disregarded him. She stroked my hair back from my forehead and kissed me gently. I can't say I minded.

After a while the doctor came. Charlie went down to let him in and apparently briefed him on the way up. He and Allie retired to the kitchen where I heard them making more coffee.

The doctor helped me remove all clothes except underpants. I'd have been much happier left alone. He tapped my joints for reflexes, peered through lights into my eyes and ears, and prodded my many sore spots. Then he sat on the stool Allie had brought, and pinched his nose.

"Concussion," he said. "Go to bed for a week."

"Don't be silly," I protested.

"Best," he said succinctly.

"But the jump jockeys get concussion one minute and ride winners the next."

"The jump jockeys are bloody fools." He surveyed me morosely. "If you'd been a jump jockey, I'd say you'd been trampled by a field of horses."

"But as I'm not?"

"Has someone been beating you?"

It wasn't the sort of question somehow that one expected one's doctor to ask. Certainly not as matter-of-factly as this.

"I don't know," I said.

"You must do."

"I agree it feels a bit like it, but if they did, I was unconscious."

"With something big and blunt," he added. "They're large bruises." He pointed to several extensive reddening patches on my thighs, arms, and trunk.

"A boot?" I said.

He looked at me soberly. "You've considered the possibility?"

"Forced on me."

He smiled. "Your friend—the one who let me in—told me you say you got drunk also while unconscious."

"Yes . . . Tube down the throat?" I suggested.

"Tell me the time factors."

I did, as nearly as I could. He shook his head dubiously. "I wouldn't have thought pouring neat alcohol straight into the stomach would produce that amount of intoxication so quickly. It takes quite a while for a large quantity of alcohol to be absorbed into the bloodstream through the stomach wall." He pondered, thinking aloud. "Two hundred and ninety milligrams, and you were maybe unconscious from the bang on the head for two hours or a little more. . . . Hmm."

He leaned forward, picked up my left forearm, and peered at it closely, front and back. Then he did the same thing with the right, and found what he was looking for.

"There," he exclaimed. "See that? The mark of a needle. Straight into the vein. They're tried to disguise it by a blow on top to bruise all the surrounding tissue. In a few more hours, the needle mark will be invisible."

"Anesthetic?" I said dubiously.

"My dear fellow. No. Probably gin."

"Gin!"

"Why not? Straight into the bloodstream. Much more efficient than a tube to the stomach. Much quicker results. And less effort, on the whole."

"But how? You can't harness a gin bottle to a hypodermic."

He grinned. "No, no. You'd set up a drip. Sterile glucose-saline drip. Standard stuff. You can buy it in plastic bags from any chemist. Just pour half a bottle of gin into one bag of solution, and drip it straight into the vein."

"But . . . how long would that take?"

"Oh, about an hour."

I thought about it. If it had been done that way, I had been transported to London with gin dripping into my system for most of the journey. There hadn't been time to do it first and set off after.

"Suppose I'd started to come round?" I asked.

"Lucky you didn't, I dare say. Nothing to stop someone bashing you back to sleep, as far as I can see."

"You take it very calmly," I said.

"So do you. And it's interesting, don't you think?"

"Oh, very," I said dryly.

7

Charlie and Allie stayed for lunch, which meant that they cooked omelets for themselves and found some reasonable cheese to follow. Out in the kitchen Charlie seemed to have been filling in gaps, because when they carried their trays into the sitting room it was clear that Allie knew all that Charlie did.

"Do you feel like eating?" Charlie asked.

"I do not."

"Drink?"

"Shut up."

"Sorry."

The body rids itself of alcohol very slowly, the doctor had said. At a rate of only ten milligrams per hour. There was no way of hastening the process and nothing much to be done about hangovers except endure them. Vitamin C, he said, helped a bit, but only if you took it in large quantities *before* drinking. Too bad, he'd said, smiling about it.

Two hundred and ninety milligrams came into the paralytic bracket. Twenty-nine hours to be rid of it. I'd lived through about ten so far. No wonder I felt so awful.

Round a mouthful of omelet Charlie said, "What are you going to do about all this?" He waved his fork from my heels to my head, still prostrate on the sofa.

"Would you suggest going to the police?" I asked neutrally.

"Er . . ."

"Exactly. The very same police who gave me hospitality last night and know for a certainty that I was so drunk that anything I might complain of could be explained away as an alcoholic delusion."

"Do you think that's why Jody and Ganser Mays did it?"

"Why else? And I suppose I should be grateful that all they did was discredit me, not bump me right off altogether."

Allie looked horrified, which was nice. Charlie was more prosaic.

"Bodies are notoriously difficult to get rid of," he said. "I would say that Jody and Ganser Mays made a rapid assessment and reckoned that dumping you drunk in London was a lot less dangerous than murder."

"There was another man as well," I said, and described my friend with sunglasses and muscles.

"Ever seen him before?" Charlie asked.

"No, never."

"The brawn of the organization?"

"Maybe he has brain, too. Can't tell."

"One thing is sure," Charlie said. "If the plan was to discredit you, your little escapade will be known all round the racecourse by tomorrow afternoon."

How gloomy, I thought. I was sure he was right. It would make going to the races more uninviting than ever.

Allie said, "I guess you won't like it, but if I were trying to drag your name through the mud, I'd've made sure there was a gossip columnist in court this morning."

"Oh, hell." Worse and worse.

"Are you just going to lie there," Charlie said, "and let them crow?"

"He's got a problem," Allie said with a smile. "How

come he was wandering around Jody's stable at that time anyway?"

"Ah," I said. "Now that's the nub of the matter, I agree. And if I tell you, you must both promise me on your souls that you will not repeat it."

"Are you serious?" Allie said in surprise.

"You don't sound it," Charlie commented.

"I am, though. Deadly serious. Will you promise?"

"You play with too many toys. It's childish."

"Many civil servants swear an oath of secrecy."

"Oh, all right," Charlie said in exasperation. "On my soul."

"And on mine," Allie said lightheartedly. "Now do get on with it."

"I own a horse called Energise," I said. They both nodded. They knew. "I spent half an hour alone with him in a crashed horse box at Sandown." They both nodded again. "Then I sent him to Rupert Ramsey, and last Sunday morning I spent half an hour alone with him again.

"So what?" Charlie said.

"So the horse at Rupert Ramsey's is not Energise."

Charlie sat bolt upright so quickly that his omelet plate fell on the carpet. He bent down, feeling around for bits of egg with his astounded face turned up to mine.

"Are you sure?"

"Definitely. He's very like him, and if I hadn't spent all that time in the crashed horse box I would never have known the difference. Owners often don't know which their horse is. It's a standing joke. But I *learnt* Energise that day at Sandown. So when I visited Rupert Ramsey's I knew he had a different horse."

"So," said Charlie slowly, "you went to Jody's stable last night to see if Energise was still there."

"Yes."

"And is he?"

"Yes."

"Absolutely certain?"

"Positive. He has a slightly Arab nose, a nick near

the tip of his left ear, a bald spot about the size of a
twopenny piece of his right shoulder. He was in box
No. Ten."

"Is that where they found you?"

"No. You remember, Allie, that we went to
Newmarket?"

"How could I forget?"

"Do you remember Hermes?"

She wrinkled her nose. "Was that a chestnut colt?"

"That's right. Well . . . I went to Trevor Kennet's
stable that day with you because I wanted to see if I
could tell whether the Hermes he had was the Hermes
Jody had had—if you see what I mean."

"And was he?" she said, fascinated.

"I couldn't tell. I found I didn't know Hermes well
enough, and anyway if Jody did switch Hermes he
probably did it before his last two races last summer,
because the horse did no good at all in those and
trailed in at the back of the field."

"Good God," Charlie said. "And did you find Hermes at Jody's place, too?"

"I don't know. There were three chestnuts there.
No markings, same as Hermes. All much alike. I
couldn't tell if any of them was Hermes. But it was in
one of the chestnut's boxes that Jody and the others
found me, and they were certainly alarmed as well as
angry."

"But what would he get out of it?" Allie asked.

"He owns some horses himself," I said. "Trainers
often do. They run them in their own names; then if
they're any good, they sell them at a profit, probably
to owners who already have horses in the stable."

"You mean," she said, "that he sent a horse he
owned himself to Rupert Ramsey, and kept Energise. Then when Energise wins another big race
he'll sell him to one of the people he trains for,
for a nice fat sum, and keep on training him himself?"

"That's about it."

"Wow."

"I'm not so absolutely sure," I said with a sardonic smile, "that he hasn't in the past sold me my own horse back after swapping it with one of his own."

"Je-*sus*," Charlie said.

"I had two bay fillies I couldn't tell apart. The first one won for a while, then turned sour. I sold her on Jody's advice and bought the second, which was one of his own. She started winning straight away."

"How are you going to prove it?" Allie said.

"I don't see how you can," said Charlie. "Especially not after this drinking charge."

We all three contemplated the situation in silence.

"Gee, dammit," said Allie, finally and explosively. "I just don't see why that guy should be allowed to rob you and make people despise you and get away with it."

"Give me time," I said mildly, "and he won't."

"Time?"

"For thinking," I explained. "If a frontal assault would land me straight into a lawsuit for slander, which it would, I'll have to come up with a sneaky scheme which will creep up on him from the rear."

Allie and Charlie looked at each other.

Charlie said to her, "A lot of the things he's invented as children's toys get scaled up very usefully."

"As if Cockerell had made the first Hovercraft for the bathtub?"

"Absolutely." Charlie nodded at her with approval. "And I dare say it was a gentle-seeming man who thought up gunpowder."

She flashed a smiling look from him to me and then suddenly looked at her watch and got to her feet in a hurry.

"Oh, golly. I'm late. I should have gone an hour ago. My sister will be so mad. Steven . . ."

Charlie looked at her resignedly and took the plates out to the kitchen. I shifted my lazy self off the sofa and stood up.

"I wish you weren't going," I said.

"I really have to."

"Do you mind kissing an unshaven drunk?"

It seemed she didn't. It was the best we'd achieved.

"The Atlantic has shrunk," I said, "since Columbus."

"Will you cross it?"

"Swim, if necessary."

She briefly kissed my bristly cheek, laughed, and went quickly. The room seemed darker and emptier. I wanted her back with a most unaccustomed fierceness. Girls had come and gone in my life, and each time afterward I had relapsed thankfully into singleness. Maybe at thirty-five, I thought fleetingly, what I wanted was a wife.

Charlie returned from the kitchen carrying a cup and saucer.

"Sit down before you fall down," he said. "You're swaying about like the Empire State."

I sat on the sofa.

"And drink this."

He had made a cup of tea, not strong, not weak, and with scarcely any milk. I took a couple of sips and thanked him.

"Will you be all right if I go?" he said. "I've an appointment."

"Of course, Charlie."

"Take care of your damned silly self."

"Yeah."

He buttoned his overcoat, gave me a sympathetic wave, and departed. Owen had long since finished changing the locks and had set off with a spare set of keys to fetch the car. I was alone in the flat. It seemed much quieter than usual.

I drank the rest of the tea, leaned back against the cushions, and shut my eyes, sick and uncomfortable from head to foot. Damn Jody Leeds, I thought. Damn and blast him to hell.

No wonder he had been so frantically determined to take Energise back with him from Sandown. He must already have had the substitute in his yard, waiting for a good moment to exchange them. When I'd said I

wanted Energise to go elsewhere immediately, he had
been ready to go to any lengths to prevent it. I was
pretty sure now that had Jody been driving the horse
box instead of Andy-Fred, I would have ended up in
the hospital if not in the morgue.

I thought about the passports that were the identity
cards of British thoroughbreds. A blank passport form
bore three stylized outlines of a horse, one from each
side and one from head-on. At the time when a foal
was named, usually as a yearling or a two-year-old, the
veterinary surgeon attending the stable where he was
being trained filled in his markings on the form, and
completed a written description alongside. The passport was then sent to the central racing authorities,
who stamped it, filed it, and sent a photocopy back to
the trainer.

I had noticed from time to time that my horses had
hardly a blaze, star, or white sock between them. It
had never struck me as significant. Thousands of horses
had no markings. I had even preferred them without.

The passports, once issued, were rarely used. As far
as I knew, apart from use in traveling abroad, they
were checked only once, which was on the day of the
horse's very first race, and that not out of suspicion,
but simply to make sure the horse actually did match
the vet's description.

I didn't doubt that the horse now standing instead of
Energise at Rupert Ramsey's stable matched Energise's
passport in every way. Details like the shape of the
nose, the slant of the stomach, the angle of the hock
wouldn't be on it.

I sighed and shifted a bit to relieve various aches.
Didn't succeed. Jody had been generous with his
boots.

I remembered with satisfaction the kicks I'd landed
in Ganser Mays's stomach. But perhaps he, too, had
taken revenge. . . .

It struck me suddenly that Jody wouldn't have had
to rely on Raymond Child to ride crooked races. Not

every time, anyway. If he had a substitute horse of poor ability, all he had to do was send him instead of the good one whenever the race had to be lost.

Racing history was packed with rumors of ringers, the good horses running in the names of the bad. Jody, I was sure, had simply reversed things and run bad horses in the names of good.

Every horse I'd owned, when I looked back, had followed much the same pattern. There would be at first a patch of sporadic success, but with regular disasters every time I staked a bundle, and then a long tail-off with no success at all. It was highly likely that the no success was due to my now having the substitute, which was running way out of its class.

It would explain why Ferryboat had run badly all autumn. Not because he resented Raymond Child's whip, but because he wasn't Ferryboat. Wrecker, too, and Hermes. And at least one of the three older horses I'd sent up North.

Five at least. that made. Also the filly. Also the first two, now sold as flops. Eight. I reckoned I might still have the real Dial. and I might still have the real Bubbleglass, because they were novices who had yet to prove their worth. But they, too, would have been matched, when they had.

A systematic fraud. All it needed was a mug.

I had been ignorantly happy. No owner expected to win all the time. and there must have been many days when Jody's disappointment, too, had been genuine. Even the best-laid bets went astray if the horses met faster opposition.

The money I'd staked with Ganser Mays had been small change compared with the value of the horses.

Impossible ever to work out just how many thousands had vanished from there. It was not only that the resale value of the substitutes after a string of bad races was low, but there was also the prize money the true horses might have won for me, and even, in the case of Hermes, the possibility of stud fees. The real Hermes might have been good enough. The substitute would fail continually as a four-year-old and no one would want to breed from him. In every way, Jody had bled every penny he could.

Energise . . .

Anger deepened in me abruptly. For Energise, I felt more admiration and affection than for any of the others. He wasn't a matter of cash value. He was the horse I'd really got to know in a horse box. One way or another, I was going to get him back.

I moved restlessly, standing up. Not wise. The headache I'd had all day began imitating a pile driver. Whether it was still alcohol or all concussion, it made little difference to the wretched end result. I went impatiently into the bedroom, put on a dressing gown over shirt and trousers, and lay down on the bed. The short December afternoon began to close in with creeping gray shadows and I reckoned it was twelve hours since Jody had dumped me in the street.

I wondered whether the doctor was right about the gin dripping into my vein. The mark he had said was a needle prick had, as predicted, vanished into a larger area of bruising. I doubted whether it had ever been there. When one thought it over, it seemed an unlikely method because of one simple snag: the improbability of Jody just happening to have a bag of saline lying around handy. Maybe it was true one could buy it from any chemist, but not in the middle of the night.

The only all-night chemists were in London. Would there have been time to belt up the M-4, buy the saline, and drip it in while parked in central London? Almost certainly not. And why bother? Any piece of rubber tubing down the throat would have done instead.

I massaged my neck thoughtfully. No soreness around the tonsils. Didn't prove anything either way.

It was still less likely that Ganser Mays, on a visit to Jody, would be around with hypodermic and drip. My absolutely stinking luck, I reflected gloomily, that I had chosen to snoop around on one of the rare evenings Jody had not been to bed by eleven. I supposed that for all my care the flash of my torch had been visible from outside. I supposed that Jody had come out of his house to see his guests off, and they'd spotted the wavering light.

Ganser Mays. I detested him in quite a different way from Jody, because I had never at any time liked him personally. I felt deeply betrayed by Jody, but the trust I'd given Ganser Mays had been a surface thing, a matter of simple expectation that he would behave with professional honor.

From Bert Huggerneck's description of the killing off of one small bookmaking business, it was probable Ganser Mays had as much professional honor as an octopus. His tentacles stretched out and clutched, and sucked the victim dry. I had a vision of a whole crowd of desperate little men sitting on their office floors because the bailiffs had taken the furniture, sobbing with relief down their telephones while Ganser Mays offered to buy the albatross of their lease for peanuts: and another vision of the same crowd of little men getting drunk in dingy pubs, trying to obliterate the pain of seeing the bright new shop fronts glowing over the ashes of their closed books.

Very likely the little men had been stupid. Very likely they should have had more sense than to believe even the most reliable-seeming information, even though the reliable-seeming information had in the past proved to be correct. Every good cardsharper knew that the victim who had been allowed to win in the beginning would part with the most in the end.

If on a minor level Ganser Mays had continually worked that trick on me, and others like me, then how much more had he stood to gain by entangling every vulnerable little firm he could find. He'd sucked the juices, discarded the husks, and grown fat.

Proof, I thought, was impossible. The murmurs of wrong information could never be traced, and the crowd of bankrupt little men probably thought of Ganser Mays as their savior, not the architect of the skids.

I imagined the sequence of events as seen by Jody and Ganser Mays when Energise ran at Sandown. To begin with, they must have decided that I should have a big bet and the horse would lose. Or even that the substitute would run instead. Right up until the day before the race, that would have been the plan. Then I refused to bet. Persuasion failed. Quick council of war. I should be taught a lesson, to bet when my trainer said so. The horse—Energise himself—was to run to win.

Fine. But Bert Huggerneck's boss went off to Sandown expecting, positively *knowing,* that Energise would lose. The only people who could have told him so were Ganser Mays and Jody. Or perhaps Raymond Child. I thought it might be informative to find out just when Bert Huggerneck's boss had been given the news. I might get Bert to ask him.

My memory wandered to Rupert Ramsey's office and the bright-orange dress of Poppet Vine. She and her husband had started to bet with Ganser Mays, and Felicity Leeds had engineered it. Did Felicity, I wondered sourly, know all about Jody's plundering ways? I supposed that she must, because she knew all their horses. Lads might come and go, discouraged by having to work too hard, but Felicity rode out twice every morning and groomed and fed in the evenings. Felicity assuredly would know if a horse had been switched.

She might be steering people to Ganser Mays out of loyalty, or for commission, or for some reason unguessed at; but everything I heard or learned seemed to make it certain that although Jody Leeds and Ganser Mays might benefit in separate ways, everything they did was a joint enterprise.

There was also, I supposed, the third man, old muscle and sunglasses. The beef of the organization. I didn't think I would ever forget him: raincoat over heavy shoulders, cloth cap over forehead, sunglasses over eyes. . . . Almost a disguise. Yet I hadn't known him. I was positive I'd never seen him anywhere before. So why had he needed a disguise at one-thirty in the morning when he hadn't expected to be seen by me in the first place?

All I knew of him was that at some point he had learned to box. That he was of sufficient standing in the trio to make his own decisions, because neither of the others had told him to hit me; he'd done it of his own accord. That Ganser Mays and Jody felt they needed his extra muscle—because neither of them was large, though Jody, in his way, was strong—in case any of the swindled victims cut up rough.

The afternoon faded and became night. All I was doing, I thought, was sorting through the implications and explanations of what had happened. Nothing at all toward getting myself out of trouble and Jody in. When I tried to plan that, all I achieved was a blank.

In the silence, I clearly heard the sound of the street door opening. My heart jumped. Pulse raced again, as in the stable. Brain came sternly afterward like a schoolmaster, telling me not to be so bloody silly.

No one but Owen had the new keys. No one but Owen would be coming in. All the same, I was relieved when the lights were switched on in the hall and I could hear his familiar tread on the stairs.

He went into the dark sitting room.

"Sir?"

"In the bedroom," I called.

He came into the doorway, silhouetted against the light in the passage.

"Shall I turn the light on?"

"No, don't bother."

"Sir . . ." His voice suddenly struck me as being odd. Uncertain. Or distressed.

"What's the matter?"

"I couldn't find the car." The words came out in a rush. The distress was evident.

"Go and get yourself a stiff drink and come back and tell me about it."

He hesitated a fraction but went away to the sitting room and clinked glasses. I fumbled around with an outstretched hand and switched on the bedside light.

Squinted at my watch. Six-thirty. Allie would be at Heathrow, boarding her airplane, waving to her sister, flying away.

Owen returned with two glasses, both containing Scotch and water. He put one glass on my bedside table and interrupted politely when I opened my mouth to protest.

"The hair of the dog. You know it works, sir."

"It just makes you drunker."

"But less queasy."

I waved toward my bedroom armchair and he sat in it easily, as before, watching me with a worried expression. He held his glass carefully, but didn't drink. With a sigh, I propped myself on one elbow and led the way. The first sip tasted vile, the second passable, the third familiar.

"Okay," I said. "What about the car?"

Owen took a quick gulp from his glass. The worried expression intensified.

"I went down to Newbury on the train and hired a taxi, like you said. We drove to where you showed me on the map, but the car didn't seem to be there. So I got the taxi-driver to go along every possible road leading away from Mr. Leeds's stable, and I still couldn't find it. The taxi-driver got pretty ratty in the end. He said there wasn't anywhere else to look. I got him to drive around in a larger area, but you said you'd walked from the car to the stables, so it couldn't have been more than a mile away, I thought."

"Half a mile, no further," I said.

"Well, sir . . . The car just wasn't there." He took another swig. "I didn't really know what to do. I got the taxi to take me to the police in Newbury, but they knew nothing about it. They rang around two or three local nicks because I made a bit of a fuss, sir, but no one down there had seen hair or hide of it."

I thought a bit. "They had the keys, of course."

"Yes, I thought of that."

"So the car could be more or less anywhere by now."

He nodded unhappily.

"Never mind," I said. "I'll report it stolen. It's bound to turn up somewhere. They aren't ordinary car thieves. When you come to think of it, we should have expected it to be gone, because if they were going to deny I had ever been in the stables last night, they wouldn't want my car found half a mile away."

"Do you mean they went out looking for it?"

"They would know I hadn't dropped in by parachute."

He smiled faintly and lowered the level in his glass to a spoonful.

"Shall I get you something to eat, sir?"

"I don't feel—"

"Better to eat. Really it is. I'll pop out to the take-away." He put his glass down and departed before I could argue, and came back in ten minutes with a wing of freshly roasted chicken.

"Didn't think you'd fancy the chips," he said. He put the plate beside me, fetched knife, fork, and napkin, and drained his own glass.

"Be going now, sir," he said. "If you're all right."

8

Whether it was Owen's care or the natural course of events, I felt a great deal better in the morning. The face peering back at me from the bathroom mirror, though adorned now with two days' stubble, had lost the gray look and the dizzy eyes. Even the bags underneath were retreating to normal.

I shaved first and bathed after, and observed that at least 20 percent of my skin was now showing bruise marks. I supposed I should have been glad I hadn't been awake when I collected them. The bothersome aches they had set up the day before had more or less abated, and coffee and breakfast helped things along fine.

The police were damping on the matter of stolen Lamborghinis. They took particulars with pessimism and said I might hear something in a week or so. Then, within half an hour, they were back on the line bristling with irritation. My car had been towed away by colleagues the night before last, because I'd parked it in a space reserved for taxis in Leicester Square. I could find it in the pound at Marble Arch, and there would be a charge for towing.

Owen arrived at nine with a long face, and was hugely cheered when I told him about the car.

"Have you seen the papers, sir?"

"Not yet."

He held out one of his own. "You'd better know," he said.

I unfolded it. Allie had been right about the gossip columnist. The paragraph was short and sharp and left no one in any doubt.

Red-face day for Steven Scott (35), wealthy race-horse owner, who was scooped by police from a Soho gutter early yesterday. At Marlborough Street Court, Scott, looking rough and crumpled, pleaded guilty to a charge of drunk and incapable. Save your sympathy. Race-followers will remember Scott recently dumped Jody Leeds (28), trainer of all his winners, without a second's notice.

I looked through my own two dailies and the *Sporting Life*. They all carried the story and in much the same vein, even if without the tabloid heat. Smug satisfaction that the kicker of underdogs had himself bitten the dust.

It was fair to assume that the story had been sent to every newspaper, and that most of them had used it. Even though I'd expected it, I didn't like it. Not a bit.

"It's bloody unfair," Owen said, reading the piece in the *Life*.

I looked at him with surprise. His usually noncommittal face was screwed into frustrated anger, and I wondered if his expression was a mirror image of my own.

"Kind of you to care."

"Can't help it, sir." The features returned more or less to normal, but with an effort. "Anything I can do, sir?"

"Fetch the car?"

He brightened a little. "Right away."

His brightness was short-lived, because he came back white-faced and angrier than I would have thought possible.

"Sir!"

"What is it?"

"The car, sir. The car."

His manner said it all. He stammered with fury over the details. The left-side front fender was crumpled beyond repair. Headlights smashed. Hub cap missing. Hood dented. All the paintwork on the left side scratched and scored down to the metal. Side door a complete write-off. Windows smashed, handle torn away.

"It looks as if it was driven against a brick wall, sir. Something like that."

I thought coldly of the side of Jody's horse box, identically damaged. My car had been smashed for vengeance.

"Were the keys in it?" I asked.

He shook his head. "It wasn't locked. Couldn't be, with one lock broken. I looked for your wallet, like you said, but it wasn't there. None of your things, sir."

"Is the car drivable?"

He calmed down a little. "Yes, the engine's all right. It must have been going all right when it was driven into Leicester Square. It looks a proper wreck, but it must be going all right; otherwise how could they have got it there?"

"That's something, anyway."

"I left it in the pound, sir. It'll have to go back to the coach builders, and they might as well fetch it from there."

"Sure," I said. I imagined he couldn't have borne to drive a crumpled car through London; he was justly proud of his driving.

Owen took his tangled emotions down to the workshop and I dealt with mine upstairs. The fresh blight Jody had laid on my life was all due to my own action in creeping into his stable by night. Had it been worth it, I wondered. I'd paid a fairly appalling price for a half-minute view of Energise: but at least I now *knew* Jody had swapped him. It was a fact, not a guess.

I spent the whole morning on the telephone straightening out the chaos. Organizing car repairs and arranging a hired substitute. Telling my bank manager and about ten assorted others that I had lost checkbook and credit cards. Assuring various inquiring relatives, who had all of course read the papers, that I was neither in jail nor dipsomaniacal. Listening to a shrill lady, whose call inched in somehow, telling me it was disgusting for the rich to get drunk in gutters. I asked her if it was okay for the poor, and if it was, why should they have more rights than I. Fair's fair, I said. Long live equality. She called me a rude word and rang off. It was the only bright spot of the day.

Last of all, I called Rupert Ramsey.

"What do you mean, you don't want Energise to run?" His voice sounded almost as surprised as Jody's at Sandown.

"I thought," I said diffidently, "that he might need more time. You said yourself he needed building up. Well, it's only a week or so to that Christmas race, and I don't want him to run below his best."

Relief distinctly took the place of surprise at the other end of the wire.

"If you feel like that, fine," he said. "To be honest, the horse has been a little disappointing on the gallops. I gave him a bit of fast work yesterday upsides a hurdler he should have made mincemeat of, and he couldn't even lie up with him. I'm a bit worried about him. I'm sorry not to be able to give you better news."

"It's all right," I said. "If you'll just keep him and do your best, that'll be fine with me. But don't run him anywhere. I don't mind waiting. I just don't want him raced."

"You made your point," he said agreeably. "What about the other two?"

"I'll leave them to your judgment. Nothing Ferryboat does will disappoint me, but I'd like to bet on Dial whenever you say he's ready."

"He's ready now. He's entered at Newbury in a fortnight. He should run very well there, I think."

"Great," I said.

"Will you be coming?" There was a load of meaning in the question. He, too, had read the papers.

"Depends on the state of my courage," I said flippantly. "Tell you nearer the day."

In the event, I went.

Most people's memories were short and I received no larger slice than I expected of the cold shoulder. Christmas had come and gone, leaving perhaps a trace of good will to all men even if they had been beastly to poor Jody Leeds and got themselves fined for drunkenness. I collected more amused sniggers than active disapproval, except of course from Quintus Leeds, who went out of his way to vent himself of his dislike. He told me again that I would certainly never be elected to the Jockey Club. Over his dead body, he said. He and Jody were both addicted to the phrase.

I was sorry about the Jockey Club. Whatever one thought of it, it was still a sort of recognition to be asked to become a member. Racing's freedom of the city—along those lines. If I had meekly allowed Jody to carry on robbing, I would have been in. As I hadn't, I was out. Sour joke.

Dial made up for a lot by winning the four-year-old hurdle by a length, and not even Quintus telling everyone it was solely due to Jody's groundwork could dim my pleasure in seeing my horse sprint to the post.

Rupert Ramsey, patting Dial's steaming sides, sounded apologetic all the same.

"Energise isn't his old self yet, I'm afraid."

Truer than you know, I thought. I said only, "Never mind. Don't run him."

He said doubtfully, "He's entered for the Champion Hurdle. I don't know if it's worth leaving him in at the next forfeit stage."

"Don't take him out," I said with haste. "I mean . . . I don't mind paying the extra entrance fee. There's always hope that he'll come right."

"Ye-es." He was unconvinced, as well he might be. "As you like, of course."

I nodded. "Drink?" I suggested.

"A quick one, then. I've some other runners."

He gulped his Scotch in friendly fashion, refused a refill, and cantered away to the saddling boxes. I wandered alone to a higher point in the stands and looked idly over the cold windy racecourse.

During the past fortnight, I'd been unable to work out just which horse was doubling for Energise. Nothing on Jody's list of horses in training seemed to match. Near-black horses were rarer than most, and none on his list were both the right color and the right age. The changeling at Rupert's couldn't be faulted on color, age, height, or general conformation. Jody, I imagined, hadn't just happened to have him lying around: he would have had to search for him diligently. How, I wondered vaguely, would one set about buying a ringer? One could hardly drift about asking if anyone knew of a spitting image at bargain prices. . . .

My wandering gaze jolted to a full stop. Down in the crowds among the rows of bookmakers' stands I was sure I had seen a familiar pair of sunglasses.

The afternoon was gray. The sky threatened snow, and the wind searched every crevice between body and soul. Not a day, one would have thought, for needing to fend off dazzle to the eyes.

There they were again. Sitting securely on the nose of a man with heavy shoulders. No cloth cap, though. A trilby. No raincoat; sheepskin.

I lifted my race glasses for a closer look. He had his back toward me, with his head slightly turned to the left. I could see a quarter-profile of one cheek and the tinted glasses that showed plainly as he looked down at a race card.

Mousy brown hair, medium length. Hands in pigskin gloves. Brownish tweed trousers. Binoculars over one shoulder. A typical racegoer among a thousand others. Except for those sun specs.

I willed him to turn round. Instead he moved away,

his back still toward me, until he was lost in the throng. Impossible to know without getting closer.

I spent the whole of the rest of the afternoon looking for a man, any man, wearing sunglasses, but the only thing I saw in shades was an actress dodging her public.

Inevitably, at one stage, I came face-to-face with Jody.

Newbury was his local meeting and he was running three horses, so I had been certain he would be there. A week earlier, I had shrunk so much from seeing him that I wanted to duck going, but in the end I had seen that it was essential. Somehow or other, I had to convince him that I had forgotten most of my nocturnal visit, that the crack on the head and concussion had, between them, wiped the memory slate clean.

I couldn't afford for him to be certain I had seen and recognized Energise and knew about the swap. I couldn't afford it for exactly the same reason that I had failed to go to the police. For the same reason that I had quite seriously sworn Charlie and Allie to secrecy.

Given a choice of prosecution for fraud and getting rid of the evidence, Jody would have jettisoned the evidence faster than sight. Energise would have been dead and dogmeat long before an arrest.

The thought that Jody had already killed him was one I tried continually to put out of my head. I reasoned that he couldn't be sure I'd seen the horse, or recognized him even if I had. They had found me down toward one end of the line of boxes; they couldn't be sure that I hadn't started at that far end and was working back. They couldn't really be sure I had been actually searching for a ringer, or even that I suspected one. They didn't know for certain why I'd been in the yard.

Energise was valuable, too valuable to destroy in needless panic. I guessed, and I hoped, that they wouldn't kill him unless they had to. Why else would they have gone to such trouble to make sure my word

would be doubted? Transporting me to London and
making me drunk had given them ample time to whisk
Energise to a safer place, and I was sure that if I'd
gone belting back there at once with the police I would
have been met by incredulous wide-eyed innocence.

"Come in, come in. Search where you like," Jody
would have said.

No Energise anywhere to be seen.

"Of course, if you were drunk, you dreamed it all,
no doubt."

End of investigation, and end of Energise, because
after that it would have been too risky to keep him.

Whereas if I could convince Jody I knew nothing, he
would keep Energise alive, and somehow or other I
might get him back.

I accidentally bumped into him outside the weighing
room. We both half turned to each other to apologize,
and recognition froze the words in our mouths.

Jody's eyes turned stormy, and I suppose mine
also.

"Get out of my bloody way," he said.

"Look, Jody," I said, "I want your help."

"I'm as likely to help you as kiss your arse."

I ignored that and put on a bit of a puzzled look.
"Did I or didn't I come to your stables a fortnight
ago?"

He was suddenly a great deal less violent, a great
deal more attentive.

"What d'you mean?"

"I know it's stupid, but somehow or other I got
drunk and collected concussion from an almighty bang
on the head, and I thought—it seemed to me that the
evening before I'd set out to visit *you*, though with
things as they are between us I can't for the *life* of me
think why. So what I'd like to know is, *did* I arrive at
your place or didn't I?"

He gave me a straight narrow-eyed stare.

"If you came, *I* never saw you," he said.

I looked down at the ground as if disconsolate and
shook my head. "I can't understand it. In the ordinary

way, I never drink much. I've been trying to puzzle it out ever since, but I can't remember *anything* between about six one evening and waking up in a police station next morning with a frightful headache and a lot of bruises. I wondered if you could tell me what I'd done in between, because as far as I'm concerned it's a blank."

I could almost feel the procession of emotions flowing out of him. Surprise, elation, relief, and a feeling that this was a totally unexpected piece of luck.

He felt confident enough to return to abuse.

"Why the bloody hell should you have wanted to visit me? You couldn't get shot of me fast enough."

"I don't know," I said glumly. "I suppose you didn't ring me up and ask me—"

"You're so right I didn't. And don't you come hanging round. I've had a bellyful of you, and I wouldn't have you back if you crawled."

He scowled, turned away, and strode off, and only because I knew what he must be really thinking could I discern the twist of satisfied smile that he couldn't entirely hide. He left me in much the same state. If he was warning me so emphatically to stay away from his stables, there was the best of chances that Energise was back there, alive and well.

I watched his sturdy backview threading through the crowd, with people smiling at him as he passed. Everyone's idea of a bright young trainer going places. My idea of a ruthless little crook.

At Christmas I had written to Allie in Code 4:

Which is the first night you could have dinner with me and where? I enclose twenty dollars for cab fare home.

On the morning after Newbury races, I received her reply, also in groups of five letters, but not in Code 4. She had jumbled her answer ingeniously enough for it to take me two minutes to unravel it. Very short messages were always the worst, and this was brief indeed.

January fifth in Miami.

I laughed aloud. And she had kept the twenty bucks.

The *Racing Calendar* came in the same post. I took it and a cup of coffee over to the big window on the balcony, and sat in an armchair there to read. The sky over the Zoo in Regent's Park looked as heavy and gray as the day before, thick with the threat of snow. Down by the canal, the bare branches of trees traced tangled black lines across the brown water and grassy banks, and the ribbon traffic as usual shattered the illusion of rural peace. I enjoyed this view of life, which, like my work, was a compromise between old primitive roots and new glossy technology. Contentment, I thought, lay in being succored by the first and cosseted by the second. If I'd had a pagan god, it would have been electricity, which sprang from the skies and galvanized machines. Mysterious lethal force of nature, harnessed and insulated and delivered on tap. My welder-uncle had made electricity seem a living person to me as a child. "Electricity will catch you if you don't look out." He said it as a warning; and I had thought of Electricity as a fiery monster hiding in the wires and waiting to pounce.

The stiff yellowish *Racing Calendar* crackled familiarly as I opened the double spread of pages and folded them back. The *Calendar,* racing's official weekly publication, contained lists of horses entered for forthcoming races, pages and pages of them, four columns to a page. The name of each horse was accompanied by the name of its owner and its trainer, and also by its age, and the weight it would have to carry if it ran.

With pencil in hand to act as insurance against skipping a line with the eye, I began painstakingly, as I

had the previous week and the week before that, to
check the name, owner, and trainer of every horse
entered in hurdle races.

Grapevine (Mrs. R. Wantage)
  B. Fritwell 6 11 11
Pirate Boy (Lord Dresden)
  A. G. Barnes 10 11 4
Hopfield (Mr. Paul Hatheleigh)
  K. Poundsgate 5 11 2

There were reams of them. I finished the Worcester
entries with a sigh. I counted 368 for one novice
hurdle and 349 for another, and not one of them what
I was looking for.

My coffee was nearly cold. I drank it anyway, and
got on with the races scheduled for Taunton.

Hundreds more names, but nothing.

Ascot, nothing. Newcastle, nothing. Warwick,
Teesside, Plumpton, Doncaster, nothing.

I put the *Calendar* down for a bit and went out onto
the balcony for some air. Fiercely cold air, slicing down
to the lungs. Primeval arctic air carrying city gunge:
the mixture as before. Over in the Park, the Zoo crea-
tures who were noisy in summer, were quiet, sheltering
in warmed houses.

Return to the task.

Huntingdon, Market Rasen, Stratford-on-Avon. . . .
I sighed before starting Stratford, and checked how
many more still lay ahead. Nottingham, Carlisle, and
Wetherby. I was in for another wasted morning, no
doubt.

Turned back to Stratford, and there it was.

I blinked and looked again carefully, as if the name
would vanish if I took my eyes off it.

Halfway down among sixty-four entries for the
Shakespeare Novice Hurdle.

Padellic (Mr. J. Leeds)
  J. Leeds 5 10 7

Padellic.

It was the first time the name had appeared in association with Jody. I knew the names of all his usual horses well, and what I had been searching for was a new one, an unknown. Owned, if my theories were right, by Jody himself. And here it was.

Nothing in the *Calendar* to show Padellic's color or markings. I fairly sprinted over to the shelf where I kept a few form books, and looked him up in every index.

Little doubt, I thought. He was listed as a black or brown gelding, five years old, a half-breed by a thoroughbred sire out of a hunter mare. He had been trained by a man I'd never heard of, and he had run three times in four-year-old hurdles without being placed.

I telephoned to the trainer at once, introducing myself as a Mr. Robinson trying to buy a cheap novice.

"Padellic?" he said in a forthright Birmingham accent. "I got rid of that bugger round October time. No bloody good. Couldn't run fast enough to keep warm. Is he up for sale again? Can't say as I'm surprised. He's a right case of the slows, that one."

"Er . . . where did you sell him?" I asked tentatively.

"Sent him to Doncaster mixed sales. Right bloody lot they had there. He fetched four hundred quid and I reckon he was dear at that. Only the one bid, you see. I reckon the bloke could've got him for three hundred if he'd tried. I was right pleased to get four for him, I'll tell you."

"Would you know who bought him?"

"Eh?" He sounded surprised at the question. "Can't say. He paid cash to the auctioneers and didn't give his name. I saw him make his bid, that's all. Big fellow. I'd never clapped eyes on him before. Wearing sunglasses. I didn't see him after. He paid up and took the horse away and I was right glad."

"What is the horse like?" I asked.

"I told you, bloody slow."

"No, I mean to look at."

"Eh? I thought you were thinking of buying him."

"Only on paper, so to speak. I thought," I lied, "that he still belonged to you."

"Oh, I see. He's black, then. More or less black, with a bit of brown round the muzzle."

"Any white about him?"

"Not a hair. Black all over. Black 'uns are often no good. I bred him, see? Meant to be bay, he was, but he turned out near black. Not a bad looker, mind. He fills the eye. But nothing there where it matters. No speed."

"Can he jump?"

"Oh, aye. In his own good time. Not bad."

"Well, thanks very much."

"You'd be buying a monkey," he said warningly. "Don't say as I didn't tell you."

"I won't buy him," I assured him. "Thanks again for your advice."

I put down the receiver reflectively. There might, of course, be dozens of large untraceable men in sunglasses going round the sales paying cash for slow black horses with no markings; and then again there might not.

The telephone bell rang under my hand. I picked up the receiver at the first ring.

"Steven?"

No mistaking that cigar-and-port voice. "Charlie."

"Have you lunched yet?" he said. "I've just got off a train round the corner at Euston, and I thought . . ."

"Here or where?" I said.

"I'll come round to you."

"Great."

He came, beaming and expansive, having invested three million somewhere near Rugby. Charlie, unlike some merchant bankers, liked to see things for himself. Reports on paper were all very well, he said, but they didn't give you the smell of a thing. If a project smelled

wrong, he didn't disgorge the cash. Charlie followed his
nose, and Charlie's nose was his fortune.

The feature in question buried itself gratefully in a
large Scotch and water.

"How about some of that nosh you gave Bert?" he
suggested, coming to the surface. "To tell you the
truth, I get tired of eating in restaurants."

We repaired amicably to the kitchen and ate bread
and bacon and curried baked beans and sausages, all
of which did no good at all to anyone's waistline, least
of all Charlie's. He patted the bulge affectionately.
"Have to get some weight off, one of these days. But
not today," he said.

We took coffee back to the sitting room and settled
comfortably in armchairs.

"I wish I lived the way you do," he said. "So easy
and relaxed."

I smiled. Three weeks of my usually quiet existence
would have driven him screaming to the madhouse. He
thrived on bustle, big business, fast decisions, financial
juggling, and the use of power. And three weeks of all
that, I thought in fairness, would drive me mad even
quicker.

"Have you made that lock yet?" he asked. He was
lighting a cigar round the words and they sounded
casual, but I wondered all of a sudden if that was why
he had come.

"Half," I said.

He shook his match to blow it out. "Let me know,"
he said.

"I promised."

He drew in a lungful of Havana and nodded, his
eyes showing unmistakably now that his mind was on
duty for his bank.

"Which would you do most for," I asked. "Friendship or the lock?"

He was a shade startled. "Depends what you want
done."

"Practical help in a counteroffensive."

"Against Jody?"

I nodded.

"Friendship," he said. "That comes under the heading of friendship. You can count me in."

His positiveness surprised me. He saw it and smiled.

"What he did to you was diabolical. Don't forget, I was here. I saw the state you were in. Saw the humiliation of that drink charge, and the pain from God knows what else. You looked a little below par, and that's a fact."

"Sorry."

"Don't be. If it was just your pocket he'd bashed, I would probably be ready with cool advice but not active help."

I hadn't expected anything like this. I would have thought it would be the other way round, that the loss of property would anger him more than the loss of face.

"If you're sure . . ." I said uncertainly.

"Of course." He was decisive. "What do you want done?"

I picked up the *Racing Calendar*, which was lying on the floor beside my chair, and explained how I'd looked for and found Padellic.

"He was bought at Doncaster sales for cash by a large man in sunglasses, and he's turned up in Jody's name."

"Suggestive."

"I'd lay this house to a sneeze," I said, "that Rupert Ramsey is worrying his guts out trying to train him for the Champion Hurdle."

Charlie smoked without haste. "Rupert Ramsey has Padellic, but thinks he has Energise. Is that right?"

I nodded.

"And Jody is planning to run Energise at Stratford-on-Avon in the name of Padellic?"

"I would think so," I said.

"So would I."

"Only it's not entirely so simple."

"Why not?"

"Because," I said, "I've found two other races for which Padellic is entered, at Nottingham and Lingfield. All the races are ten to fourteen days ahead, and there's no telling which Jody will choose."

He frowned. "What difference does it make which he chooses?"

I told him.

He listened with his eyes wide open and the eyebrows disappearing upward into his hair. At the end, he was smiling.

"So how do you propose to find out which race he's going for?" he asked.

"I thought," I said, "that we might mobilize your friend Bert. He'd do a lot for you."

"What, exactly?"

"Do you think you could persuade him to apply for a job in one of Ganser Mays's betting shops?"

Charlie began to laugh. "How much can I tell him?"

"Only what to look for. Not why."

"You slay me, Steven."

"And another thing," I said. "How much do you know about the limitations of working hours for truck drivers?"

9

Snow was falling when I flew out of Heathrow, thin scurrying flakes in a driving wind. Behind me I left a half-finished lock, a half-mended car, and a half-formed plan.

Charlie had telephoned to say Bert Huggerneck had been taken on at one of the shops formerly owned by his ex-boss, and I had made cautious inquiries from the auctioneers at Doncaster. I'd had no success. They had no record of the name of the person who'd bought Padellic. Cash transactions were common. They couldn't possibly remember who had bought one particular cheap horse three months earlier. End of inquiry.

Owen had proclaimed himself as willing as Charlie to help in any way he could. Personal considerations apart, he said, whoever had bent the Lamborghini deserved hanging. When I came back, he would help me build the scaffold.

The journey from snow to sunshine took eight hours. Seventy-five degrees at Miami Airport and only a shade cooler outside the hotel on Miami Beach; and it felt great. Inside the hotel, the air-conditioning brought things nearly back to an English winter, but my sixth-floor room faced straight toward the afternoon sun. I drew back the closed curtains and opened the window, and let heat and light flood in.

Below, round a glittering pool, tall palm trees swayed in the sea wind. Beyond, the concrete edge to the hotel grounds led immediately down to a narrow strip of sand and the frothy white waves edging the Atlantic. with mile upon mile of deep-blue water stretching away to the lighter-blue horizon.

I had expected Miami Beach to be garish and was unprepared for its beauty. Even the ranks of huge white slab hotels, with rectangular windows piercing their façades in a uniform geometrical pattern, had a certain grandeur, punctuated and softened as they were by scattered palms.

Round the pool, people lay in rows on day beds beside white-fringed sun umbrellas, soaking up ultra-violet like a religion. I changed out of my travel-sticky clothes and went for a swim in the sea, paddling lazily in the warm January water and sloughing off cares. Jody Leeds was five thousand miles away, in another world. Easy, and healing, to forget him.

Upstairs again, showered and dressed in slacks and cotton shirt, I checked my watch for the time to telephone Allie. After the letters, we had exchanged cables, though not in code because the cable company didn't like it.

I had sent: "What address Miami."

She had replied: "Telephone four two six eight two three nine after six any evening."

When I called her, it was five past six on January 5th, local time. The voice that answered was not hers, and for a soggy moment I wondered if Western Union had jumbled the message, as it often did, and that I should never find her.

"Miss Ward? Do you mean Miss Alexandra?"

"Yes," I said with relief.

"Hold the line, please."

After a pause came the familiar voice, remembered but suddenly fresh. "Hello?"

"Allie . . . It's Steven."

"Hi." Her voice was laughing. "I've won almost fifty dollars, *if* you're in Miami."

"Collect it," I said.

"I don't believe it."

"We have a date," I said reasonably.

"Oh, sure."

"Where do I find you?"

"Twelve twenty-four Garden Island," she said. "Any taxi will bring you. Come right out; it's time for cocktails."

Garden Island proved to be a shady offshoot of land with wide enough channels surrounding it to justify its name. The cab rolled slowly across twenty yards of decorative iron bridge and came to a stop outside 1224. I paid off the driver and rang the bell.

From the outside, the house showed little. The whitewashed walls were deeply obscured by tropical plants and the windows by metal screens. The door itself looked solid enough for a bank.

Allie opened it. Smiled widely. Gave me a noncommittal kiss.

"This is my cousin's house," she said. "Come in."

Behind its secretive front, the house was light and large and glowing with clear uncomplicated colors. Blue, sea green, bright pink, white, and orange.

"My cousin Minty," Allie said, "and her husband, Warren Barbo."

I shook hands with the cousins. Minty was neat, dark, and utterly self-possessed in lemon-colored beach pajamas. Warren was large, sandy, and full of noisy good humor. They gave me a tall, iced unspecified drink and led me into a spacious glass-walled room for a view of the setting sun.

Outside in the garden, the yellowing rays fell on a lush lawn, a calm pool, and white plastic lounging chairs. All peaceful and prosperous and a million miles from blood, sweat, and tears.

"Alexandra tells us you're interested in horses," Warren said, making hostlike conversation. "I don't know how long you plan on staying, but there's a race meet at Hialeah right now, every day this week. And the bloodstock sales, of course, in the evenings. I'll be going myself some nights and I'd be glad to have you along."

The idea pleased me, but I turned to Allie.

"What are your plans?"

"Millie and I split up," she said without visible regret. "She said when we were through with Christmas and New Year's she would be off to Japan for a spell, so I grabbed a week down here with Minty and Warren."

"Would you come to the races, and the sales?"

"Sure."

"I have four days," I said.

She smiled brilliantly but without promise. Several other guests arrived for drinks at that point, and Allie said she would fetch the canapés. I followed her to the kitchen.

"You can carry the stone crabs," she said, putting a large dish into my hands. "And okay, after a while we can sneak out and eat someplace else."

For an hour I helped hand round those understudies for a banquet, American-style canapés. Allie's delicious work. I ate two or three and, like a true male chauvinist, meditated on the joys of marrying a good cook.

I found Minty at my side, her hand on my arm, her gaze following mine.

"She's a great girl," she said. "She swore you would come."

"Good," I said with satisfaction.

"She told us to be careful what we said to you, because you always understood the implications, not just the words. And I guess she was right."

"You've only told me that she wanted me to come, and thought I liked her enough to do it."

"Yeah, but . . ." She laughed. "She didn't actually say all that."

"I see what you mean."

She took out of my hands a dish of thin pastry boats filled with pink chunks of lobster in pale-green mayonnaise. "You've done more than your duty here," she said, smiling. "Get on out."

She lent us her car. Allie drove it northward along the main boulevard of Collins Avenue and pulled up at a restaurant called Stirrup and Saddle.

"I thought you might feel at home here," she said teasingly.

The place was crammed. Every table in sight was taken, and, as in many American restuarants, the tables were so close together that only emaciated waiters could inch around them. Blowups of racing scenes decorated the walls, and saddles and horseshoes abounded.

Dark décor, loud chatter, and, to my mind, too much light.

A slightly harassed headwaiter intercepted us inside the door.

"Do you have reservations, sir?"

I began to say I was sorry, as there were dozens of people already waiting round the bar, when Allie interrupted.

"Table for two, name of Barbo."

He consulted his lists, smiled, nodded. "This way, please."

There was miraculously after all one empty table, tucked in a corner but with a good view of the busy room. We sat comfortably in dark wooden-armed chairs and watched the headwaiter turn away the next customers decisively.

"When did you book this table?" I asked.

"Yesterday. As soon as I got down here." The white teeth gleamed. "I got Warren to do it; he likes this place. That's when I made the bets. He and Minty said it was crazy, you wouldn't come all the way from England just to take me out to eat."

"And you said I sure was crazy enough for anything."

"I certainly did."

We ate bluepoint oysters and barbecued baby ribs and salads. Noise and clatter from other tables washed around us and waiters towered above with huge loaded trays. Business was brisk.

"Do you like it here?" Allie asked, tackling the ribs.

"Very much."

She seemed relieved. I didn't add that some quiet candlelight would have done even better. "Warren says all horse people like it, as he does."

"How horsy is Warren?"

"He owns a couple of two-year-olds. Has them in training with a guy in Aiken, South Carolina. He was hoping they'd be running here at Hialeah, but they've both got chipped knees and he doesn't know if they'll be any good any more."

"What are chipped knees?" I asked.

"Don't you have chipped knees in England?"

"Heaven knows."

"So will Warren." She dug into the salad, smiling down at the food. "Warren's business is real estate but his heart beats out there where the hoofs thunder along the homestretch."

"Is that how he puts it?"

Her smile widened. "It sure is."

"He said he'd take us to Hialeah tomorrow, if you'd like."

"I might as well get used to horses, I suppose." She spoke with utter spontaneity, and then in a way stood back and looked at what she'd said. "I m-mean . . ." she stammered.

"I know what you mean," I said, smiling.

"You always do, dammit."

We finished the ribs and progressed to coffee. She asked how fast I'd recovered from the way she had seen me last, and what had happened since. I told her about the gossip columns and the car, and she was fiercely indignant—mostly about the car.

"But it was so beautiful!"

"It will be again."

"I'd like to murder that Jody Leeds."

She scarcely noticed, that time, that she was telling me what she felt for me. The sense of a smoothly deepening relationship filled me with contentment.

After three cups of dawdled coffee, I paid the bill and we went out to the car.

"I can drop you off at your hotel," Allie said. "It's quite near here."

"Certainly not. I'll see you safely home."

She grinned. "There isn't much danger. All the alligators in Florida are a hundred miles away in the Everglades."

"Some alligators have two feet."

"Okay, then." She drove slowly southward. Outside her cousin's house, she put on the hand brake but left the engine running.

"You'd better borrow this car to go back. Minty won't mind."

"No, I'll walk."

"You can't. It's all of four miles."

"I like seeing things close. Seeing how they're made and I'll follow Collins Avenue so I won't get lost."

"You *are* nuts."

I switched off the engine, put my arm around her shoulders, and kissed her the same way as at home, several times. She sighed deeply, but not, it seemed, with boredom.

I hired an Impala in the morning and drove down to Garden Island. A cleaner answered the door and showed me through to where Warren and Minty were in swimsuits, standing by the pool in January sunshine as warm as July back home.

"Hi," said Minty in welcome. "Alexandra said to tell you she'll be right back. She's having her hair fixed."

The fixed hair, when it appeared, looked as smooth and shining as the girl underneath. A black-and-tan sleeveless cotton dress did marvelous things for her waist and stopped in plenty of time for the legs. I imagine appreciation was written large on my face, because a wide smile broke out as soon as she saw me.

We sat by the pool drinking cold fresh orange juice while Warren and Minty changed into street clothes. The day seemed an interlude, a holiday, to me, but not to the Barbos. Warren's life, I came to realize, was along the lines of perpetual summer vacation interrupted by short spells in the office. Droves of sharp young men did the legwork of selling dream retirement homes to elderly sun-seekers, and Warren, the organizer, went to the races.

Hialeah Turf Club was a sugar-icing racecourse, as pretty as lace. Miami might show areas of cracks and rust and sun-pceled poverty on its streets, but in the big green park in its suburb the lush life survived and seemingly flourished.

Bright birds in cages beguiled visitors the length of the paddock, and a decorative pint-sized railway trundled around. Tons of ice cream added to weight problems, and torn-up pari-mutuel tickets fluttered to the ground like snow.

The racing itself that day was moderate, which didn't prevent me losing my bets. Allie said it served me right, gambling was a nasty habit on a par with jumping off cliffs.

"And look where it's got you," she pointed out.

"Where?"

"In Ganser Mays's clutches."

"Not any more."

"Which came first," she said, "the gamble or the race?"

"All life's a gamble. The fastest sperm fertilizes the egg."

She laughed. "Tell that to the chickens."

It was the sort of day when nonsense made sense. Minty and Warren met relays of drinking pals and left us much alone, which suited me fine, and at the end of the racing program we sat high up on the stands looking over the course while the sunlight died to yellow and pink and scarlet. Drifts of flamingos on the small lakes in the center of the track deepened from pale pink to intense rose, and the sky on the water reflected silver and gold.

"I bet it's snowing in London," I said.

After dark and after dinner, Warren drove us round to the sales paddock on the far side of the racecourse, where spotlights lit a scene that was decidedly more rustic than the stands. Sugar icing stopped with the tourists: horse-trading had its feet on the grass.

There were three main areas linked by short undefined paths and well-patronized open-fronted bars: the sale ring, the parade ring, and long barns lined with stalls, where the merchandise ate hay and suffered prods and insults and people looking at its teeth.

Warren opted for the barns first, and we wandered down the length of the nearest while he busily consulted his catalogue. Minty told him they were definitely not buying any more horses until the chipped knees were all cleared up. No, dear, Warren said soothingly, but with a gleam in his eye that spelled death to the bank balance.

I looked at the offerings with interest. A mixed bunch of horses that had been raced, from three years upward. Warren said the best sales were those for two-year-olds at the end of the month, and Minty said why didn't he wait awhile and see what they were like.

The lights down the far end of the barn were dim, and the horse in the last stall of all was so dark that at first I thought the space was empty. Then an eye shimmered, and a movement showed a faint gleam on a rounded rump.

A black horse; black like Energise.

I looked at him first because he was black, and then more closely, with surprise. He was indeed very like Energise. Extremely like him.

The likeness abruptly crystallized an idea I'd already been turning over in my mind. The horse was a gift from the gods, and who was I to look it in the mouth?

"What have you found?" Warren asked, advancing with good humor.

"I've a hurdler like this at home."

Warren looked at the round label stuck onto one hindquarter, which bore the number 62.

"Hip Number Sixty-two," he said, flicking the pages of the catalogue. "Here it is. Black Fire, five-year-old gelding. Humph." He read quickly down the page through the achievements and breeding. "Not much good, and never was much good, I guess."

"Pity."

"Yeah." He turned away. "Now there's a damned nice-looking chestnut colt along there."

"No, Warren," said Minty despairingly.

We all walked back to look at the chestnut colt. Warren knew no more about buying horses than I did, and besides the first thing I'd read on page 1 of the catalogue was the clear warning that the auctioneers didn't guarantee the goods were of merchantable quality. In other words, if you bought a lame duck it was your own silly fault.

"Don't pay any attention to that," said Warren expansively. "As long as you don't take the horse out of the sales paddock, you can get a veterinarian to check a horse you've bought, and if he finds anything wrong you can call the deal off. But you have to do it within twenty-four hours."

"Sounds fair."

"Sure. You can have X-rays even. Chipped knees would show on an X-ray. Horses can walk and look okay with chipped knees, but they sure can't race."

Allie said with mock resignation, "So what exactly are chipped knees?"

Warren said, "Cracks and compressions at the ends of the bones at the knee joint."

"From falling down?" Allie asked.

Warren laughed kindly. "No. From too much hard galloping on dirt. The thumping does it."

I borrowed the sales catalogue from Warren again, for a deeper look at the regulations, and found the twenty-four-hour inspection period applied only to broodmares, which wasn't much help. I mentioned it diffidently to Warren. "It says here," I said, "that it's wise to have a vet look at a horse for soundness before you bid. After is too late."

"Is that so?" Warren retrieved his book and peered at the small print. "Well, I guess you're right." He received the news good-naturedly. "Just shows how easy it is to go wrong at horse sales."

"And I hope you remember it," Minty said with meaning.

Warren did in fact seem a little discouraged from his chestnut colt, but I wandered back for a second look at Black Fire and found a youth in jeans and grubby sweat shirt bringing him a bucket of water.

"Is this horse yours?" I asked.

"Nope. I'm just the help."

"Which does he do most, bite or kick?"

The boy grinned. "Reckon he's too lazy for either."

"Would you take him out of that dark stall so I could have a look at him in the light?"

"Sure." He untied the halter from the tethering ring and brought Black Fire out into the central alley, where the string of electric lights burned without much effect down the length of the barn.

"There you go," he said, persuading the horse to arrange its legs as if for a photograph. "Fine-looking fella, isn't he?"

"What you can see of him," I said.

I looked at him critically, searching for differences. But there was no doubt he was the same. Same height, same elegant shape, even the same slightly dished Arab-looking nose. And black as coal, all over. When I walked up and patted him, he bore it with fortitude. Maybe his sweet nature, I thought. Or maybe tranquilizers.

On the neck or head of many horses, the hair grows in one or more whorls, making a pattern that is entered as an identifying mark on the passports. Energise had no whorls at all. Nor had Padellic. I looked carefully at the forehead, cheeks, neck, and shoulders of Black Fire, and ran my fingers over his coat. As far as I could feel or see in that dim light, there were no whorls on him either.

"Thanks a lot," I said to the boy, stepping back.

He looked at me with surprise. "You don't mean to look at his teeth or feel his legs?"

"Is there something wrong with them?"

"I guess not."

"Then I won't bother," I said, and left unsaid the truth understood by us both, that even if I'd inspected those extremities I wouldn't have been any the wiser.

"Does he have a tattoo number inside his lip?" I asked.

"Yeah, of course." The surprise raised his eyebrows to peaks, like a clown. "Done when he first raced."

"What is it?"

"Well, gee, I don't know." His tone said he couldn't be expected to, and no one in his senses would have bothered to ask.

"Take a look."

"Well, okay." He shrugged and with the skill of practice opened the horse's mouth and turned down the lower lip. He peered closely for a while, during which time the horse stood suspiciously still, and then let him go.

"Far as I can see, there's an F and a six and some others, but it's not too light in here and anyway the numbers get to go fuzzy after a while, and this fella's five now, so the tatoo would be all of three years old."

"Thanks anyway."

"You're welcome." He pocketed my offered five dollars and took the very unfiery Black Fire back to his stall.

I turned to find Allie, Warren, and Minty standing in a row, watching. Allie and Minty both wore indulgent feminine smiles and Warren was shaking his head.

"That horse has won a total of nine thousand three hundred and twenty-six dollars in three years' racing," he said. "He won't have paid the feed bills." He held out the catalogue, opened at Black Fire's page, and I took it and read the vaguely pathetic race record for myself.

"At two, unplaced. At three, three wins, four times third. At four, twice third. Total: three wins, six times third, earned $9,326."

A modest success as a three-year-old, but all in fairly low-class races. I handed the catalogue back to Warren with a smile of thanks, and we moved unhurriedly out of that barn and along to the next. When even Warren had had a surfeit of peering into stalls, we went outside and watched the first entries being led into the small wooden-railed collecting ring.

A circle of lights round the rails lit the scene, aided by spotlights set among the surrounding trees. Inside, as on a stage, small bunches of people were anxiously adding the finishing touches of gloss that might wring a better price from the unperceptive. Some of the horses' manes were decorated with a row of bright wool pompons, arching along the top of the neck from ears to withers as if the horses were ready for the circus. Hip No. 1, resplendent in scarlet pompons, raised his long bay head and whinnied theatrically.

I told Allie and the Barbos I would be back in a minute, and left them leaning on the rails. A couple of inquiries and one misdirection found me standing in the cramped office of the auctioneers in the sale-ring building.

"A report from the veterinarian? Sure thing. Pay in advance, please. If you don't want to wait, return for the report in half an hour."

I paid and went back to the others. Warren was deciding it was time for a drink, and we stood for a

while in the fine warm night near one of the bars
drinking Bacardi and Coke out of throwaway cartons.

Brilliant light poured out of the circular sales building in a dozen places through open doors and slatted
windows. Inside, the banks of canvas chairs were beginning to fill up, and down on the rostrum in the
center the auctioneers were shaping up to start the
evening's business. We finished the drinks, duly threw
away the cartons, and followed the crowd into the
show.

Hip No. 1 waltzed in along a ramp and circled the
rostrum with all his pompons nodding. The auctioneer
began his singsong selling, amplified and insistent, and
to me, until my ears adjusted, totally unintelligible. Hip
No. 1 made five thousand dollars, and Warren said the
prices would all be low because of the economic situation.

Horses came and went. When Hip No. 15, in orange
pompons, had fetched a figure that had the crowd
murmuring in excitement, I slipped away to the office
and found that the veterinary surgeon himself was
there, dishing out his findings to other inquirers.

"Hip Number Sixty-two?" he echoed. "Sure, let me
find my notes." He turned over a page or two in a
notebook. "Here we are. Dark bay or brown gelding,
right?"

"Black," I said.

"Uh-uh. Never say black." He smiled briefly, a busy
middle-aged man with the air of a clerk. "Five years.
Clean bill of health." He shut the notebook and turned
to the next customer.

"Is that all?" I said blankly.

"Sure," he said briskly. "No heart murmur, legs
cool, teeth consistent with given age, eyes normal,
range of movement normal, trots sound. No bowed
tendons, no damaged knees."

"Thanks," I said.

"You're welcome."

"Is he tranquilized?"

He looked at me sharply, then smiled. "I guess so. Acepromazine, probably."

"Is that usual, or would he be a rogue?"

"I wouldn't think he'd had much. He should be okay."

"Thanks again."

I went back to the sale ring in time to see Warren fidgeting badly over the sale of the chestnut colt. When the price rose to fifteen thousand, Minty literally clung onto his hands and told him not to be a darned fool.

"He must be sound," Warren protested, "to make that money."

The colt made twenty-five thousand in thirty seconds' brisk bidding and Warren's regrets rumbled on all evening. Minty relaxed as if the ship of state had safely negotiated a killing reef and said she would like a breath of air. We went outside and leaned again on the collecting-ring rails.

There were several people from England at the sales. Faces I knew, faces that knew me. No close friends; scarcely acquaintants; but people who would certainly notice and remark if I did anything unexpected.

I turned casually to Warren.

"I've money in New York," I said. "I can get it tomorrow. Would you lend me some tonight?"

"Sure," he said good-naturedly, fishing for his wallet. "How much do you need?"

"Enough to buy that black gelding."

"What?" His hand froze and his eyes widened.

"Would you buy it for me?"

"You're kidding."

"No."

He looked at Allie for help. "Does he mean it?"

"He's crazy enough for anything," she said.

"That's just what it is," Warren said. "Crazy. Crazy to buy some goddamned useless creature just because he looks like a hurdler you've got back home."

To Allie this statement suddenly made sense. She

smiled vividly and said, "What are you going to do with him?"

I kissed her forehead. "I tend to think in circles," I said.

10

Warren, enjoying himself hugely, bought Back Fire for $4,600. Bid for it, signed for it, and paid for it.

With undiminished good nature, he also contracted for its immediate removal from Hialeah and subsequent shipment by air to England.

"Having himself a ball," Minty said.

His good spirits lasted all the way back to Garden Island and through several celebratory nightcaps.

"You sure bought a stinker," he said cheerfully. "But boy, I haven't had so much fun in years. Did you see that guy's face, the one I bid against? He thought he was getting it for a thousand." He chuckled. "At four thousand five he sure looked mad, and he could see I was going on forever."

Minty began telling him to make the most of it, it was the last horse he'd be buying for a long time, and Allie came to the door to see me off. We stood outside for a while in the dark, close together.

"One day down. Three to go," she said.

"No more horses," I promised.

"Okay."

"And fewer people."

A pause. Then again, "Okay."

I smiled and kissed her good night and pushed her

indoors before my best intentions should erupt into good old-fashioned lust. The quickest way to lose her would be to move too fast.

She said how about the Florida Keys and how about a swim and how about a picnic. We went in the Impala with a cold box of goodies in the trunk and the tropic of Cancer flaming away over the horizon ahead.

The highway to Key West stretched for mile after mile across a linked chain of causeways and small islands. Palm trees, sand dunes, sparkling water, and scrubby grass. Few buildings. Sun-bleached wooden huts; wooden landing stages; fishing boats. Huge skies, hot sun, vast seas. Also Geryhound buses on excursions and noisy families in station wagons, with Mom in pink plastic curlers.

Allie had brought directions from Warren about one of the tiny islands where he fished, and when we reached it we turned off the highway onto a dusty side road that was little more than a track. It ended abruptly under two leaning palms, narrowing to an Indian-file path through sand dunes and tufty grass toward the sea. We took the picnic box and walked, and found ourselves surprisingly in a small sandy hollow from which neither the car nor the road could be seen.

"That," said Allie, pointing at the sea, "is Hawk Channel."

"Can't see any hawks."

"You'd want cooks in Cook Strait."

She took off the loose white dress she'd worn on the way down and dropped it on the sand. Underneath she wore a pale-blue-and-white bikini, and underneath that warm honey-colored skin.

She took the skin without more ado into the sea, and I stripped off shirt and trousers and followed her. We swam in the free warm-cool water and it felt the utmost in luxury.

"Why are these islands so uninhabited?" I asked.

"Too small, most of them. No fresh water. Hurricanes, as well. It isn't always so gentle here. Sizzling hot in the summer, and terrible storms."

The wind in the palm treetops looked as if butter wouldn't melt in its mouth. We splashed in the shallows and walked up the short beach to regain the warm little hollow, Allie delivering on the way a fairly nonstop lecture about turtles, bonefish, marlin, and tarpon. It struck me in the end that she was talking fast to hide that she was feeling self-conscious.

I fished in my jacket pocket and brought out a twenty-dollar bill.

"Bus fare home," I said, holding it out to her.

She laughed a little jerkily. "I still have the one you sent from England."

"Did you bring it?"

She smiled, shook her head, took the note from me, folded it carefully, and pushed it into the wet top half of her bikini.

"It'll be safe there," she said matter-of-factly. "How about a vodka martini?"

She had brought drinks, ice, and delicious food. The sun in due course shifted thirty degrees round the sky, and I lay lazily basking in it while she put the empties back in the picnic box and fiddled with spoons.

"Allie?"

"Mmm?"

"How about now?"

She stopped the busy rattling. Sat back on her heels. Pushed the hair out of her eyes, and finally looked at my face.

"Try sitting here," I said, patting the sand beside me with an unemphatic palm.

She tried it. Nothing cataclysmic seemed to happen to her in the way of fright.

"You've done it before," I said persuasively, stating a fact.

"Yeah . . . but . . ."

"But what?"

"I didn't really like it."

"Why not?"

"I don't know. I didn't like the guy enough, I expect."

"Then why the hell sleep with him?"

"You make it sound so simple. But at college—well, one sort of had to. Three years ago, most of one summer. I haven't done it since. I've been not exactly afraid to, but afraid I would . . . be unfair. . . ." She stopped.

"You can catch a bus whenever you like," I said.

She smiled, and bit by bit lay down beside me. I knew she wouldn't have brought me to this hidden place if she hadn't been willing at least to try. But acquiescence, in view of what she'd said, was no longer enough. If she didn't enjoy it, I couldn't.

I went slowly, giving her time. A touch. A kiss. An undemanding smoothing of hand over skin. She breathed evenly, trusting but unaroused.

"Clothes off?" I suggested. "No one can see us."

". . . Okay."

She unhitched the bikini top, folded it over the twenty dollars, and put it on the sand beside her. The pants followed in a moment. Then she sat with her arms wrapped round her knees, staring out to sea.

"Come on," I said, smiling, my shorts joining hers. "The fate worse than death isn't all that bad."

She laughed and lay down beside me, and it seemed as if she'd made up her mind to do her best, even if she found it unsatisfactory. But in a while she gave the first uncontrollable shiver of authentic pleasure, and after that it became not just all right but very good indeed.

"Oh, God," she said in the end, half laughing, half gasping for air. "I didn't know . . ."

"Didn't know what?" I said, sliding lazily down beside her.

"At college . . . he was clumsy. And too quick."

She stretched out her hand, fumbled in the bikini, and picked up the twenty-dollar bill.

She waved it in the air, holding it between finger and thumb. Then she opened her hand, and the wind blew her fare home away along the beach.

11

London was cold enough to encourage emigration. I arrived back early Tuesday morning with sand in my shoes and sympathy for Eskimos, and Owen collected me, his face pinched and blue.

"We've had snow and sleet and the railways are on strike," he said, putting my suitcase in the hired Cortina. "Also the mild steel you ordered hasn't come and there's a cobra loose somewhere in Regent's Park."

"Thanks very much."

"Not at all, sir."

"Anything else?"

"A Mr. Kennet rang from Newmarket to say Hermes has broken down. And . . . sir . . ."

"What?" I prompted, trying to dredge up resignation.

"Did you order a load of manure, sir?"

"Of course not."

The total garden in front of my house consisted of three tubs of fuchsia, an old walnut tree, and several square yards of paving slabs. At the rear, nothing but workshop.

"Some has been delivered, sir."

"How much?"

"I can't see the dustmen moving it."

He drove steadily from Heathrow to home, and I dozed from the jet-lag feeling that it was midnight.

When we stopped, it was not in the driveway but out on the road, because the driveway was completely blocked by a dunghill five feet high.

It was even impossible to walk round it without it sticking to one's shoes. I crabbed sidewise with my suitcase to the door, and Owen drove off to find somewhere else to park.

Inside, on the mat, I found the delivery note. A postcard, handwritten in ball-point capitals, short and unsweet.

"SHIT TO THE SHIT."

Charming little gesture. Hardly original, but disturbing all the same, because it spoke so eloquently of the hatred prompting it.

Felicity? I wondered.

There was something remarkably familiar about the consistency of the load. A closer look revealed half-rotted horse droppings mixed with a little straw and a lot of sawdust. Straight from a stable muck heap, not from a garden supplier: and if it looked exactly like Jody's own familiar muck heap, that wasn't in itself conclusive. I dared say one vintage was much like another.

Owen came trudging back and stared at the smelly obstruction in disgust.

"If I hadn't been using the car to go home, like you said, I wouldn't have been able to get out of the garage this morning to fetch you."

"When was it dumped?"

"I was here yesterday morning, sir. Keeping an eye on things. Then this morning I called round to switch on the central heating, and there it was."

I showed him the card. He looked, read, wrinkled his nose in distaste, but didn't touch.

"There'll be fingerprints on that, I shouldn't wonder."

"Do you think it's worth telling the police?" I asked dubiously.

"Might as well, sir. You never know—this nutter might do something else. I mean, whoever went to all this trouble is pretty sick."

"You're very sensible, Owen."

"Thank you, sir."

We went indoors and I summoned the constabulary, who came in the afternoon, saw the funny side of it, and took away the card in polyethylene.

"What are we going to do with the bloody stuff?" said Owen morosely. "No one will want it on their flower beds, it's bung-full of undigested hayseeds, and that means weeds."

"We'll shift it tomorrow."

"There must be a ton of it." He frowned gloomily.

"I didn't mean spadeful by spadeful," I said. "Not you and I. We'll hire a grab."

Hiring things took the rest of the day. Extraordinary what one could hire if one tried. The grab proved to be one of the easiest on a long list.

At about the time merchant bankers could reasonably be expected to be reaching for their hats, I telephoned to Charlie.

"Are you going straight home?" I asked.

"Not necessarily."

"Care for a drink?"

"On my way," he said.

When he arrived, Owen took his Rover to park it, and Charlie stood staring at the muck heap, which looked no more beautiful under the streetlights and was, moreover, beginning to ooze round the edges.

"Someone doesn't love me," I said with a grin. "Come on in and wipe your feet rather thoroughly on the mat."

"What a stink."

"Lavatory humor," I agreed.

He left his shoes alongside mine on the tray of newspaper Owen had prudently positioned near the front door, and followed me upstairs in his socks.

"Who?" he said, shaping up to a large Scotch.

"A shit is what Jody's wife Felicity called me after Sandown."

"Do you think she did it?"

"Heaven knows. She's a capable girl."

"Didn't anyone see the—er—delivery?"

"Owen asked the neighbors. No one saw a thing. No one ever does in London. All Owen discovered was that the muck wasn't there at seven yesterday evening when the man from two doors along let his Labrador make use of my fuchsia tubs."

He drank his whiskey and asked what I'd done in Miami. I couldn't stop the smile coming. "Besides that," he said.

"I bought a horse."

"You're a glutton for punishment."

"An understudy," I said. "For Energise."

"Tell all to your Uncle Charlie."

I told, if not all, most.

"The trouble is, though, that although we must be ready for Saturday at Stratford, he might choose Nottingham on Monday or Lingfield on Wednesday," I said.

"Or none of them."

"And it might freeze."

"How soon would we know?" Charlie asked.

"He'll have to declare the horse to run four days before the race, but he then has three days to change his mind and take him out again. We wouldn't know for sure until the runners are published in the evening papers the day before. And even then we need the nod from Bert Huggerneck."

He chuckled. "Bert doesn't like the indoor life. He's itching to get back on the racecourse."

"I hope he'll stick to the shop."

"My dear fellow!" Charlie lit a cigar. "Bert's a great scrapper by nature, and if you could cut him in on the real action he'd be a lot happier. He's taken a strong dislike to Ganser Mays, and he says that for a capitalist you didn't seem half bad. He knows there's something afoot, and he said if there's a chance of anyone punching Ganser Mays on the long bleeding nose he would like it to be him."

I smiled at the verbatim reporting. "All right. If he really feels like that, I do indeed have a job for him."

"Doing what?"

"Directing the traffic."

He puffed at the cigar. "Do you know what your plan reminds me of?" he said. "Your own Rola toys. There you are, turning the single handle, and all the little pieces will rotate on their spindles and go through their allotted acts."

"You're no toy," I said.

"Of course I am. But at least I know it. The real trick will be programing the ones who don't."

"Do you think it will all work?"

He regarded me seriously. "Given ordinary luck, I don't see why not."

"And *you* don't have moral misgivings?"

His sudden huge smile warmed like a fire. "Didn't you know that merchant bankers are pirates under the skin?"

Charlie took Wednesday off and we spent the whole day prospecting the terrain. We drove from London to Newbury. from Newbury to Stratford-on-Avon, from Stratford to Nottingham, and from Nottingham back to Newbury. By that time the bars were open, and we repaired to the Chequers for revivers.

"There's only the one perfect place," Charlie said, "and it will do for both Stratford and Nottingham."

I nodded. "By the fruit stall."

"Settle on that, then?"

"Yes."

"And if he isn't down to run at either of those courses, we spend Sunday surveying the road to Lingfield?"

"Right."

"I haven't felt so alive since my stint in the army.

However this turns out, I wouldn't have missed it for the world," he said.

His enthusiasm was infectious and we drove back to London in good spirits.

Things had noticeably improved in the garden. The muck heap had gone, and Owen had sloshed to some effect with buckets of water, though without obliterating the smell. He had also stayed late, waiting for my return. All three of us left our shoes in the hall and went upstairs.

"Too Japanese for words," Charlie said.

"I stayed, sir," Owen said, "because a call came from America."

"Miss Ward?" I said hopefully.

"No, sir. About a horse. It was a shipping firm. They said a horse consigned to you would be on a flight to Gatwick Airport tonight as arranged. Probable time of arrival, 10 A.M. tomorrow morning. I wrote it down." He pointed to the pad beside the telephone. "But I thought I would stay in case you didn't see it. They said you would need to engage transport to have the horse met."

"You will be meeting it," I said.

"Very good, sir," he said calmly.

"Owen," Charlie said, "if he ever kicks you out, come to me."

We all sat for a while discussing the various arrangements and Owen's part in them. He was as eager as Charlie to make the plan work, and he, too, seemed to be plugged into some inner source of excitement.

"I'll enjoy it, sir," he said, and Charlie nodded in agreement. I had never thought of either of them as being basically adventurous, and I had been wrong.

I was wrong also about Bert Huggerneck, and even in a way about Allie, for they, too, proved to have more fire than reservations.

Charlie brought Bert with him after work on Thursday and we sat round the kitchen table poring over a large-scale map.

"That's the A-34," I said, pointing with a pencil to a

red line running south to north. "It goes all the way
from Newbury to Stratford. For Nottingham, you
branch off just north of Oxford. The place we've chosen is some way south of that. Just here . . ." I marked
it with the pencil. "About a mile before you reach the
Abingdon by-pass."

"I know that bleeding road," Bert said. "Goes past
the Harwell atomic."

"That's right."

"Yeah. I'll find that. Easy as dolly-birds."

"There's a roadside fruit stall there," I said. "Shut,
at this time of year. A sort of wooden hut."

"Seen dozens of 'em," Bert said, nodding.

"It has a good big space beside it for cars."

"Which side of the road?"

"On the near side, going north."

"Yeah. I get you."

"It's on a straight stretch after a fairly steep hill.
Nothing will be going very fast there. Do you think you
could manage?"

"Here," he complained to Charlie. "That's a bleeding insult."

"Sorry," I said.

"Is that all I do, then? Stop the traffic?" He sounded
disappointed; and I'd thought he might need to be
persuaded.

"No," I said. "After that, you do a lot of hard work
extremely quickly."

"What, for instance?"

When I told him, he sat back on his chair and
positively beamed.

"That's more bleeding like it," he said. "Now that's a
daisy, that is. Now you might think I'm slow on my
feet, like, with being big, but you'd be bleeding
wrong."

"I couldn't do it all without you."

"Hear that?" he said to Charlie.

"It might even be true," Charlie said.

Bert at that point described himself as peckish, and
moved in a straight line to the storage cupboard.

"What've you got here, then? Don't you ever *eat?* Do you want this tin of ham?"

"Help yourself," I said.

Bert made a sandwich inch-deep in mustard, and ate it without blinking. A couple of cans of beer filled the cracks.

"Can I chuck the betting shop, then?" he asked between gulps.

"What have you learned about Ganser Mays?"

"He's got a bleeding nickname—that's one thing I've learned. A couple of smart young managers run his shops now; you'd never know they was the same place. All keen and sharp and not a shred of soft heart like my old boss."

"A softhearted bookmaker?" Charlie said. "There's no such thing."

"Trouble was," Bert said, ignoring him, "he had a soft head and all."

"What is Ganser Mays's nickname?" I asked.

"Eh? Oh, yeah. Well, these two smart alecks, who're sharp enough to cut themselves, they call him Squeezer. Squeezer Mays. When they're talking to each other, of course, that is."

"Squeezer because he squeezes people like your boss out of business?"

"You don't hang about, do you? Yeah, that's right. There's two sorts of squeezer. The one they did on my boss, telling him horses were fixed to lose when they wasn't. And the other way round, when the smart alecks know a horse that's done no good before is fixed to win. Then they go round all the little men putting thousands on, a bit here and a bit there, and all the little men think it's easy pickings, because they think the bad horse can't win in a month of bleeding Sundays. And then of course it does, and they're all down the bleeding drain."

"They owe Ganser Mays something like the national debt."

"That's right. And they can't raise enough bread. So then Mr. pious bleeding Mays comes along and says he'll be kind and take the shop to make up the difference . Which he does."

"I thought small bookies were more clued up nowadays." I said.

"You'd bleeding well think so, wouldn't you? They'll tell you they are, but they bleeding well aren't. Oh, sure, if they find afterwards there's been a right fiddle, like, they squeal blue murder and refuse to pay up, but take the money in the first place—of course they do. Like innocent little lambs."

"I don't think there would be any question of anyone thinking it a fiddle this time," I said.

"There you are, then. Quite a few would all of a bleeding sudden be finding they were swallowed up by that smarmy bastard. Just like my poor old boss."

I reflected for a minute or two. "I think it would be better if you stayed in the betting shop until we're certain which day the horse is going to run. I don't imagine they would risk letting him loose without backing him, so we must suppose that his first race is *it*. But, if possible, I'd like to be sure. And you might hear something if you're still in the shop."

"Keep my ears flapping, you mean?"

"Absolutely. And eyes open."

"Philby won't have nothing on me," Bert said.

Charlie stretched out to the makings of the sandwich and assembled a smaller edition for himself.

"Now, transport," I said. "I've hired all the vehicles we need from a firm in Chiswick. I was there this morning, looking them over. Owen took a Land-Rover and trailer from there to Gatwick to meet Black Fire and ferry him to his stable, and he's coming back by train. Then there's the caravan for you, Charlie, and the car to pull it. Tomorrow, Owen is driving those to Reading and leaving them in the station car park, again coming back by train. I got two sets of keys for the car and caravan, so I'll give you yours now." I went through to the sitting room and came back with the small jingling bunch. "Whichever day we're off, you can go down to Reading by train and drive from there."

"Fine," Charlie said, smiling broadly.

"The caravan is one they hire out for horse shows and exhibitions and things like that. It's fitted out as a sort of office. No beds or cookers—just a counter, a couple of desks, and three or four folding chairs. Owen and I will load it with all the things you'll need before he takes it to Reading."

"Great."

"Finally, there's the big van for Owen. I'll bring that here tomorrow and put the shopping in it. Then we should be ready."

"Here," said Bert. "How's the cash, like?"

"Do you want some, Bert?"

"It's only—well, seeing as how you're hiring things left, right, and center—well, I wondered if it wouldn't be better to hire a car for me, too, like. Because my old banger isn't all that bleeding reliable, see? I wouldn't like to miss the fun because of a boiling bleeding radiator or some such."

"Sure," I said. "Much safer." I went back to the sitting room, fetched some cash, and gave it to Bert.

"Here," he said. "I don't need that much. What do you think I'm going to hire, a golden coach?"

"Keep it anyway."

He looked at me dubiously. "I'm not doing this for bread, mate."

I felt humbled. "Bert . . . give me back what you don't use. Or send it to the Injured Jockeys' Fund."

His face lightened. "I'll take my old boss down the boozer a few times. Best bleeding charity there is!"

Charlie finished his sandwich and wiped his fingers on his handkerchief. "You won't forget the sign-writing, will you?" he said.

"I did it today," I assured him. "Want to see?"

We trooped down to the workshop, where various painted pieces of the enterprise were standing around drying.

"Blimey," Bert said. "They look bleeding real."

"They'd have to be," Charlie said, nodding.

"Here," Bert said. "Seeing these makes it seem—well, as if it's all going to happen."

Charlie went home to a bridge-playing wife in an opulent detached in Surrey and Bert to the two-up two-down terraced he shared with his fat old mum in Staines. Some time after their departure, I got the car out and drove slowly down the M-4 to Heathrow.

I was early. About an hour early. I had often noticed that I tended to arrive prematurely for things I was looking forward to, as if by being there early one could make them happen sooner. It worked in reverse that time. Allie's airplane was half an hour late.

"Hi," she said, looking as uncrushed as if she'd traveled a few miles, not a few thousand. "How's cold little old England?"

"Warmer since you're here."

The wide smile had lost none of its brilliance, but now there was also a glow in the eyes, where the Miami sun shone from within.

"Thanks for coming," I said.

"I wouldn't miss this caper for the world." She gave me a kiss full of excitement and warmth. "And I haven't told my sister I'm here."

"Great," I said with satisfaction; and took her home to the flat.

The change of climate was external. We spent the night, our first together, warmly entwined under a goose-feather quilt: more comfortable, more relaxed, and altogether more cozy than the beach or the fishing boat or my hotel bedroom on an air-conditioned afternoon in Miami.

We set off early next morning while it was still dark, shivering in the chill January air and impatient for the car heater to make an effort. Allie drove, concentrating fiercely on the left-hand business, telling me to watch out that she didn't instinctively turn the wrong way at crossings. We reached the fruit stall on the A-34 safely in two hours, and drew up there in the wide sweep of

car-parking space. Huge lorries ground past on the
main route from the docks at Southampton to the
heavy-industry area at Birmingham—a road, in places,
still too narrow for its traffic.

Each time a heavy truck breasted the adjoining hill
and drew level with us, it changed its gears, mostly
with a good deal of noise. Allie raised her voice. "Not
the quietest of country spots."

I smiled. "Every decibel counts."

We drank hot coffee from a thermos flask and
watched the slow gray morning struggle from gloomy
to plain dull.

"Nine o'clock," said Allie, looking at her watch.
"The day starts late in these parts."

"We'll need you here by nine," I said.

"You just tell me when to start."

"Okay."

She finished her coffee. "Are you certain he'll come
this way?"

"It's the best road, and the most direct, and he
always does."

"One thing about having an ex-friend for an ene-
my," she said. "You know his habits."

I packed away the coffee, and we started again,
turning south.

"This is the way you'll be coming," I said. "Straight
up the A-34."

"Right."

She was driving now with noticeably more confidence, keeping left without the former steady frown of
anxiety. We reached a big crossroads and stopped at
the traffic lights. She looked around and nodded.
"When I get here, there'll only be a couple of miles to
go."

We pressed on for a few miles, the road climbing
and descending over wide stretches of bare downlands,
bleak and windy and uninviting.

"Slow down a minute," I said. "See that turning
there, to the left? That's where Jody's stables are.
About a mile along there."

"I really hate that man," she said.

"You've never met him."

"You don't have to know snakes to hate them."

We went round the Newbury by-pass, Allie screwing her head round alarmingly to learn the route from the reverse angle.

"Okay," she said. "Now what?"

"Still the A-34. Signposts to Winchester. But we don't go that far."

"Right."

Through Whitchurch, and six miles beyond, we took a narrow side road on the right, and in a little while turned in to the drive of a dilapidated-looking country house with a faded paint job on a board at the gate.

HANTSFORD MANOR RIDING SCHOOL.

FIRST-CLASS INSTRUCTION. RESIDENTIAL ACCOMMO-DATION.

PONIES AND HORSES FOR HIRE OR AT LIVERY.

I had chosen it from an advertisement in the *Horse and Hound* because of its location, to make the drive from there to the fruit stall as simple as possible for Allie, but now that I saw it, I had sinking doubts.

There was an overall air of life having ended, of dust settling, weeds growing, wood rotting, and hope dead. Exaggerated, of course. Though the house indoors smelled faintly of fungus and decay, the proprietors were still alive. They were two much-alike sisters, both about seventy, with thin wiry bodies, dressed in jodhpurs, hacking jackets, and boots. They both had kind faded blue eyes, long strong lower jaws, and copious iron-gray hair in businesslike hair nets.

They introduced themselves as Miss Johnston and Mrs. Fairchild-Smith. They were glad to welcome Miss Ward. They said they hoped her stay would be comfortable. They never had many guests at this time of year. Miss Ward's horse had arrived safely the day before, and they were looking after him.

"Yourselves?" I asked doubtfully.

"Certainly ourselves." Miss Johnston's tone dared me to imply they were incapable. "We always cut back on staff at this time of year."

They took us out to the stables, which, like everything else, were suffering from advancing years, and moreover appeared to be empty. Among a ramshackle collection of wooden structures, whose doors any self-respecting toddler could have kicked down, were three or four brick-built boxes in a sturdy row; in one of these we found Black Fire.

He stood on fresh straw. There was clean water in his bucket and good-looking hay in his net, and he had his head down to the manger, munching busily at oats and bran. All too clear to see where any profits of the business disappeared: into the loving care of the customers.

"He looks fine," I said, and to myself, with relief, confirmed that he was indeed the double of Energise, and that in the warm distant Miami night I hadn't been mistaken.

Allie cleared her throat. "Er . . . Miss Johnston, Mrs. Fairchild-Smith. Tomorrow morning I may be taking Black Fire over to some friends, to ride with them. Would that be okay?"

"Of course," they said together.

"Leaving at eight o'clock?"

"We'll see he's ready for you, my dear," said Miss Johnston.

"I'll let you know for sure when I've called my friends. If I don't go tomorrow, it may be Monday, or Wednesday."

"Whenever you say, my dear." Miss Johnston paused delicately. "Could you give us any idea how long you'll be staying?"

Allie said, without hesitation, "I guess a week's board would be fair, both for Black Fire and me, don't you think? We may not be here for all of seven days, but obviously at this time of year you won't want to be bothered with shorter reservations."

The sisters looked discreetly pleased, and when Allie produced cash for the bulk of the bill in advance, a faint flush appeared on their thin cheeks and narrow noses.

"Aren't they the weirdest?" Allie said as we drove out of the gates. "And how do you shift these damned gears?"

She sat, this time, at the wheel of the Land-Rover I'd hired from Chiswick, learning her way round its unusual levers.

"That one with the red knob engages four-wheeled drive, and the yellow one is for four ultra-low gears, which you shouldn't need, as we're not aiming to cross plowed fields or drag tree stumps out of the ground."

"I wouldn't rule them out when you're around."

She drove with growing ease, and before long we returned to hitch on the two-horse trailer. She had never driven with a trailer before, and reversing, as always, brought the worst problems. After a fair amount of swearing on all sides and the best part of an hour's trundling around Hampshire, she said she guessed she would reach the fruit stall if it killed her. When we returned to Hantsford Manor after refueling, she parked with the Land-Rover's nose already facing the road, so that at least she wouldn't louse up the linkage, as she put it, before she'd even started.

"You'll find the trailer a good deal heavier with a horse in it," I said.

"You don't say."

We returned to Black Fire, without encountering the sisters, and I produced from an inner pocket a haircutting gadget in the form of a razor blade incorporated into a comb.

"What are you going to do with that?" Allie said.

"If the two old girls materialize, keep them chatting," I said. "I'm just helping the understudy to look like the star."

I went into the box and as calmly as possible approached Black Fire. He wore a head-collar but was not tied up, and the first thing I did was attach him to the tethering chain. I ran my hand down his neck and patted him a few times and said a few soothing nonsenses. He didn't seem to object to my presence, so rather gingerly I laid the edge of the haircutting comb against his black coat.

I had been told often that nervous people made horses nervous also. I wondered if Black Fire could feel my fumbling inexperience. I thought that after all this I would really have to spend more time with horses, that owning them should entail the obligation of intimacy.

His muscles twitched. He threw his head up and down. He whinnied. He also stood fairly still, so that when I'd finished my delicate scraping he had a small bald patch on his right shoulder, the same size and in the same place as the one on Energise.

Allie leaned her elbows on the closed bottom half of the stable door and watched through the open top half.

"Genius," she said, smiling, "is nine-tenths an infinite capacity for taking pains."

I straightened, grinned, patted Black Fire almost familiarly, and shook my head. "Genius is infinite pain," I said. "I'm happy. Too bad."

"How do you know, then? About genius being pain?"

"Like seeing glimpses of a mountain from the valley."

"And you'd prefer to suffer on the peaks?"

I let myself out of the loose-box and carefully fastened all the bolts.

"You're either issued with climbing boots or you aren't," I said. "You can't choose. Just as well."

The sisters reappeared and invited us to take sherry: a double thimbleful in unmatched cut glasses. I looked at my watch and briefly nodded, and Allie asked if we might use the telephone to call the friends.

In the library, they said warmly. This way. Mind the hole in the carpet. Over there, on the desk. They smiled, nodded, and retreated.

Beside the telephone stood a small metal box with a stuck-on notice: *"Please pay for calls."* I dialed the London number of the Press Association and asked for the racing section.

"Horses knocked out of the novice hurdle at Stratford?" said a voice. "Well, I suppose so, but we prefer people to wait for the evening papers. These inquiries waste our time."

"Arrangements to make as soon as possible," I murmured.

"Oh, all right. Wait a sec. Here we are." He read out about seven names rather fast. "Got that?"

"Yes, thank you very much," I said.

I put down the telephone slowly, my mouth suddenly dry. Jody had declared Padellic as a Saturday Stratford runner three days ago. If he had intended not to go there, he would have had to remove his name by a Friday-morning deadline of eleven o'clock. . . .

Eleven o'clock had come and gone. None of the horses taken out of the novice hurdle had been Padellic.

"Tomorrow," I said. "He runs tomorrow."

"Oh." Allie's eyes were wide. "Oh, my."

12

Eight o'clock, Saturday morning.

I sat in my hired Cortina in a lay-by on the road over the top of the Downs, watching while the drizzly dawn took the eyestrain out of the passing head-lights.

I was there much too early, because I hadn't been able to sleep. The flurry of preparations all Friday afternoon and evening had sent me to bed still in top gear, and from then on my brain had whirred re-lentlessly, thinking of all the things that could go wrong.

Snatches of conversations drifted back.

Rupert Ramsey expressing doubts and amazement on the other end of the telephone.

"You want to do *what?*"

"Take Energise for a ride in a horse box. He had a very upsetting experience in a horse box at Sandown, in a crash. . . . I thought it might give him confidence to go for an uneventful drive."

"I don't think it would do much good," he said.

"All the same, I'm keen to try. I've asked a young chap called Pete Duveen, who drives his own box, just to pick him up and take him for a ride. I thought tomorrow would be a good day. Pete Duveen says he can collect him at seven-thirty in the morning. Would you have the horse ready?"

"You're wasting your money," he said regretfully. "I'm afraid there's more wrong with him than nerves."

"Never mind. And . . . will you be at home tomorrow evening?"

"After I get back from Chepstow races, yes."

The biggest race meeting of the day was scheduled for Chepstow. The biggest prizes were on offer there, and most of the top trainers like Rupert would be going.

"I hope you won't object," I said, "but after Energise returns from his ride, I'd like to hire a security firm to keep an eye on him."

Silence from the other end. Then his voice, carefully polite: "What on earth for?"

"To keep him safe," I said reasonably. "Just a guard to patrol the stable and make regular checks. The guard wouldn't be a nuisance to anybody."

I could almost feel the shrug coming down the wire along with the resigned sigh. Eccentric owners should be humored. "If you want to, I suppose. . . . But why?"

"If I called at your house tomorrow evening," I suggested, "I could explain."

"Well . . ." He thought for a bit. "Look, I'm having a few friends to dinner. Would you care to join us?"

"Yes, I would," I said. "I'd like that very much."

I yawned in the car, and stretched. Despite anorak, gloves, and thick socks, the cold encroached on fingers and toes, and through the drizzle-wet windows the bare rolling Downs looked thoroughly inhospitable. Straight ahead through the windshield wipers, I could see a good two miles of the A-34. It came over the brow of a distant hill opposite, swept down into a large valley, and rose again, higher still, to cross the Downs at the point where I sat.

A couple of miles to my rear lay the crossroads with the traffic lights, and a couple of miles beyond that the fruit stall.

Bert Huggerneck, wildly excited, had telephoned at six the evening before.

"Here, know what? There's a squeezer on tomorrow!"

"On Padellic?" I said hopefully.

"What else? On bleeding little old Padellic."

"How do you know?"

"Listened at the bleeding door," he said cheerfully. "The two smart alecks was talking. Stupid bleeding gits. All over the whole bleeding country, Ganser Mays is going to flood the little bookies' shops with last-minute bets on Padellic. The smart alecks are all getting their girl friends, what the little guys don't know by sight, to go round putting on the dough. Hundreds of them, by the sound of it."

"You're a wonder, Bert."

"Yeah," he said modestly. "Missed my bleeding vocation."

Owen and I had spent most of the afternoon loading the big hired van from Chiswick and checking that we'd left nothing out. He worked like a demon, all energy and escaping smiles.

"Life will seem flat after this," he said.

I had telephoned Charlie from Hantsford Manor and caught him before he went to lunch.

"We're off," I said. "Stratford, tomorrow."

"Tally bloody ho!"

He rang me from his office again at five. "Have you seen the evening papers?"

"Not yet," I said.

"Jody has two definite runners at Chepstow as well."

"Which ones?"

"Cricklewood in the big race and Asphodel in the handicap chase."

Cricklewood and Asphodel both belonged to the same man, who, since I'd left, had become Jody's

No. 1 owner. Cricklewood was now also ostensibly the best horse in the yard.

"That means," I said, "that Jody himself will almost certainly go to Chepstow."

"I should think so," Charlie agreed. "He wouldn't want to draw attention to Padellic by going to Stratford, would you think?"

"No, I wouldn't."

"Just what we wanted," Charlie said with satisfaction. "Jody going to Chepstow."

"We thought he might."

Charlie chuckled. *"You* thought he might." He cleared his throat. "See you tomorrow, in the trenches. And, Steven . . ."

"Yes?"

"Good luck with turning the handle."

Turning the handle . . .

I looked at my watch. Still only eight-thirty and too early for any action. I switched on the car's engine and let the heater warm me up.

All the little toys revolving on their spindles, going through their programed acts. Allie, Bert, Charlie, and Owen. Felicity and Jody Leeds, Ganser Mays. Padellic and Energise and Black Fire. Rupert Ramsey and Pete Duveen.

And one little toy I knew nothing about.

I stirred, thinking of him uneasily.

A big man who wore sunglasses. Who had muscles, and knew how to fight.

What else?

Who had bought Padellic at Doncaster sales.

I didn't know if he had bought the horse after Jody had found it, or if he knew Energise well enough to look for a double himself; and there was no way of finding out.

I'd left no slot for him in today's plan. If he turned up like a joker, he might entirely disrupt the game.

I picked up my race glasses, which were lying on the seat beside me, and started watching the traffic crossing

the top of the opposite distant hill. From two miles
away, even with strong magnification, it was difficult to
identify particular vehicles, and in the valley and climbing the hill straight toward me they were head-on and
foreshortened.

What looked like a car and trailer came over the
horizon. I glanced at my watch. If it was Allie, she was
dead on time.

I focused on the little group. Watched it down into
the valley. Definitely a Land-Rover and animal trailer.
I got out of the car and watched it crawling up the hill,
until finally I could make out the number plate. Definitely Allie.

Stepping a pace onto the road, I flagged her down.
She pulled into the lay-by, opened her window, and
looked worried.

"Is something wrong?"

"Not a thing." I kissed her. "I got here too early, so
I thought I'd say good morning."

"You louse. When I saw you standing there waving,
I thought the whole darned works were all fouled
up."

"You found the way, then."

"No problems."

"Sleep well?"

She wrinkled her nose. "I guess so. But oh, boy,
that's some crazy house. Nothing works. If you want to
flush the john, you have to get Miss Johnston. No one
else has the touch. I guess they're really sweet, though,
the poor old dears."

"Shades of days gone by," I said.

"Yeah, that's exactly right. They showed me their
scrapbooks. They were big in the horse world thirty-
forty years ago. Won things at shows all over. Now
they're struggling on a fixed income and I guess they'll
soon be starving."

"Did they say so?"

"Of course not. You can see it, though."

"Is Black Fire all right?"

"Oh, sure. They helped me load him up, which was

lucky because I sure would have been hopeless on my own."

"Was he any trouble?"

"Quiet as a little lamb."

I walked round to the back of the trailer and looked in over the three-quarter door. Black Fire occupied the left-hand stall. A full hay net lay in the right. The ladies might starve, but their horses wouldn't.

I went back to Allie. "Well . . ." I said. "Good luck."

"To you, too."

She gave me the brilliant smile, shut the window, and with care pulled out of the lay-by into the stream of northbound traffic.

Time and timing, the two essentials.

I sat in the car metaphorically chewing my nails and literally looking at my watch every half-minute.

Padellic's race was the last of the day, the sixth race, the slot often allotted to that least crowd-pulling of events, the novice hurdle. Because of the short January afternoons, the last race was scheduled for three-thirty.

Jody's horses, like those of most other trainers, customarily arrived at a racecourse about two hours before they were due to run. Not often later, but quite often sooner.

The journey by horse box from Jody's stable to Stratford-on-Avon racecourse took two hours. The very latest, therefore, that Jody's horse box would set out would be eleven-thirty.

I thought it probable it would start much sooner than that. The latest time allowed little margin for delays on the journey or snags on arrival, and I knew that if I were Jody and Ganser Mays and had so much at stake, I would add a good hour for contingencies.

Ten-thirty . . . But suppose it was earlier. . . .

I swallowed. I had had to guess.

If for any reason Jody had sent the horse very early and it had already gone, all our plans were for nothing.

If he had sent it the day before . . . If he had sent it with another trainer's horses, sharing the cost . . . If for some unimaginable reason the driver took a different route . . .

The "if"s multiplied like stinging ants.

Nine-fifteen.

I got out of the car and extended the aerial of a large efficient walkie-talkie. No matter that British civilians were supposed to have permission in triple triplicate before operating them: in this case we would be cluttering the air for seconds only, and lighting flaming beacons on hilltops would have caused a lot more fuss.

"Charlie?" I said, transmitting.

"All fine here."

"Great." I paused for five seconds, and transmitted again. "Owen?"

"Here, sir."

"Great."

Owen and Charlie could both hear me, but they couldn't hear each other, because of the height of the Downs where I sat. I left the aerial extended and the switches to "receive," and put the gadget back in the car.

The faint drizzle persisted, but my mouth was dry.

I thought about the five of us, sitting and waiting. I wondered if the others, like me, were having trouble with their nerves.

The walkie-talkie crackled suddenly. I picked it up.

"Sir?"

"Owen?"

"Pete Duveen just passed me."

"Fine."

I could hear the escaping tension in my own voice and the excitement in his. The on-time arrival of Pete Duveen signaled the real beginning. I put the walkie-talkie down again and was disgusted to see my hand shaking.

Pete Duveen in his horse box drove into the lay-by nine and a half minutes after he had passed Owen, who was stationed in sight of the road to Jody's stable. Pete owned a pale-blue horse box with his name, address, and telephone number painted in large black-and-red letters on the front and back. I had seen the box and its owner often at race meetings, and it was he, in fact, whom I had engaged at Sandown on my abortive attempt to prevent Jody taking Energise home.

Pete Duveen shut down his engine and jumped from the cab.

"Morning, Mr. Scott."

"Morning," I said, shaking hands. "Glad to see you."

"Anything to oblige." He grinned cheerfully, letting me know both that he thought I was barmy and also that I had every right to be, as long as I was harmless and, moreover, paying him.

He was well-built and fair, with weather-beaten skin and a threadbare mustache. Open-natured, sensible, and honest. A one-man transport firm, and making a go of it.

"You brought my horse?" I said.

"Sure thing."

"And how has he traveled?"

"Not a peep out of him the whole way."

"Mind if I take a look at him?" I said.

"Sure thing," he said again. "But honest, he didn't act up when we loaded him and I wouldn't say he cared a jimmy riddle one way or another."

I unclipped and opened the side part of the horse box that formed the entrance ramp for the horses. It was a bigger box than Jody's, but otherwise much the same. The horse stood in the front row of stalls in the one furthest across from the ramp, and he looked totally uninterested in the day's proceedings.

"You never know," I said, closing the box again.

"He might be all the better for the change of routine."

"Maybe," Pete said, meaning he didn't think so.

I smiled. "Like some coffee?"

"Sure would."

I opened the trunk of my car, took out a thermos, and poured us each a cup.

"Sandwich?" I offered.

Sandwich accepted. He ate beef-and-chutney hungrily. "Early start," he said, explaining his hunger. "You said to get here soon after nine-thirty."

"That's right," I agreed.

"Er . . . why so early?"

"Because," I said reasonably, "I've other things to do all the rest of the day."

He thought me even nuttier, but the sandwich plugged the opinion in his throat.

The sky began to brighten and the tiny-dropped drizzle dried away. I talked about racing in general and Stratford-on-Avon in particular, and wondered how on earth I was to keep him entertained if Jody's box should, after all, not leave home until the last possible minute.

By ten-fifteen we had drunk two cups of coffee each and he had run out of energy for sandwiches. He began to move restively and make ready-for-departure signs, of which I blandly took no notice. I chatted on about the pleasures of owning race horses and my stomach bunched itself into anxious knots.

Ten-twenty. Ten-twenty-five. Ten-thirty. Nothing.

It had all gone wrong, I thought. One of the things that could have sent everything awry had done so.

Ten-thirty-five.

"Look," Pete said persuasively. "You said you had a great deal to do today, and honestly, I don't think—"

The walkie-talkie crackled.

I practically leaped toward the front of the car and reached in for it.

"Sir?"

"Yes, Owen."

"A blue horse box just came out of his road and turned south."

"Right."

I stifled my disappointment. Jody's two runners setting off to Chepstow, no doubt.

"What's that?" Pete Duveen said, his face appearing at my shoulder full of innocent inquiry.

"Just a radio."

"Sounded like a police car."

I smiled and moved away back to the rear of the car, but I had hardly got Pete engaged again in useless conversation when the crackle was repeated.

"Sir?"

"Go ahead."

"A fawn-colored box with a red slash, sir. Just turned north." His voice trembled with excitement.

"That's it, Owen."

"I'm on my way."

I felt suddenly sick. Took three deep breaths. Pressed the transmit button.

"Charlie?"

"Yes."

"The box is on its way."

"Halle-bloody-lujah."

Pete was again looking mystified and inquisitive. I ignored his face and took a traveling bag out of the trunk of my car.

"Time to go," I said pleasantly. "I think, if you don't mind, I'd like to see how my horse behaves while going along, so could you start the box now and take me up the road a little way?"

He looked very surprised, but then he had found the whole expedition incomprehensible.

"If you like," he said helplessly. "You're the boss."

I made encouraging signs to him to get into his cab and start the engine, and while he was doing it I stowed my bag on the passenger side. The diesel engine whirred and coughed and came to thunderous life, and I went back to the Cortina.

Locked the trunk, shut the windows, took the keys, locked the doors, and stood leaning against the fender, holding binoculars in one hand and walkie-talkie in the other.

Pete Duveen had taken nine and a half minutes from Jody's road to my lay-by, and Jody's box took exactly the same. Watching the far hill through race glasses, I saw the big dark blue van that contained Owen come over the horizon, followed almost immediately by an oblong of fawn.

Watched them down into the valley and onto the beginning of the hill.

I pressed the transmit button.

"Charlie?"

"Go ahead."

"Seven minutes. Owen's in front."

"Right."

I pushed down the aerial of the walkie-talkie and took it and myself along to the passenger door of Pete's box. He looked across and down at me inquiringly, wondering why on earth I was still delaying.

"Just a moment," I said, giving no explanation, and he waited patiently, as if humoring a lunatic.

Owen came up the hill, changed gears abreast of the lay-by, and slowly accelerated away. Jody's horse box followed, doing exactly the same. The scrunched left-side front had been hammered out, I saw, but respraying lay in the future. I had a quick glimpse into the cab: two men, neither of them Jody, both unknown to me. A box driver who had replaced Andy-Fred, and the lad with the horse. Couldn't be better.

I hopped briskly up into Pete's box.

"Off we go, then."

My sudden haste looked just as crazy as the former dawdling, but again he made no comment and merely did what I wanted. When he had found a gap in the traffic and pulled out onto the road, there were four or five vehicles between Jody's box and ourselves, and this seemed to me a reasonable number.

I spent the next four miles trying to look as if nothing in particular were happening while listening to my heart beat like a discothèque. Owen's van went through the traffic lights at the big crossroads a half-second before they changed to amber, and Jody's box came to a halt as they showed red. The back of Owen's van disappeared round a bend in the road.

Between Jody's box and Pete's there were three private cars and one small van belonging to an electrical firm. When the lights turned green, one of the cars peeled off to the left and I began to worry that we were getting too close.

"Slow down just a fraction," I suggested.

"If you like . . . but there's not a squeak from the horse." He glanced over his shoulder to where the black head looked patiently forward through a small observation hatch, as nervous as a suet pudding.

A couple of private cars passed us. We motored sedately onward, and came to the bottom of the next hill. Pete changed his gear smoothly and we lumbered noisily up. Near the top, his eye took in a notice board on a tripod at the side of the road.

"Damn," he said.

"What is it?" I asked.

"Did you see that?" he said. "Census point ahead."

"Never mind, we're not in a hurry."

"I suppose not."

We breasted the hill. The fruit stall lay ahead on our left, with the sweep of car park beside it. Down the center of the road stood a row of the red-and-white cones used for marking road obstructions, and in the northbound lane, directing the traffic, stood a large man in navy-blue police uniform with a black-and-white checked band round his cap.

As we approached he waved the private cars past and then directed Pete into the fruit-stall car park,

walking in beside the horse box and talking to him
through the window.

"We'll keep you only a few minutes, sir. Now, will
you pull right round in a circle and park facing me
just here, sir?"

"All right," Pete said resignedly, and followed
the instructions. When he pulled the brake on, we were
facing the road. On our left, about ten feet away,
stood Jody's box, but facing in the opposite direction.
On the far side of Jody's box was Owen's van. And
beyond Owen's van, across about twenty yards of cin-
dery park, lay the caravan, its long flat windowless side
toward us.

The Land-Rover and trailer that Allie had brought
stood near the front of Jody's box. There was also the
car hitched to the caravan, and the car Bert had hired,
and all in all the whole area looked populated, official,
and busy.

A second large notice on a tripod faced the car park
from just outside the caravan.

DEPARTMENT OF THE ENVIRONMENT. CENSUS POINT.

And near a door at one end of the caravan a further
notice on a stand said "Way In."

Jody's horse-box driver and Jody's lad were following its directions, climbing the two steps up to the caravan, and disappearing within.

"Over there, please, sir." A finger pointed authori-
tatively. "And take your driving license and logbook,
please."

Pete shrugged, picked up his papers, and went.
I jumped out and watched him go.

The second he was inside, Bert slapped me on
the back in a most unpoliceman-like way and said,
"Easy as Blackpool tarts."

We zipped into action. Four minutes maximum,
and a dozen things to do.

I unclipped the ramp of Jody's horse box and

let it down quietly. The one thing that would bring any horse-box driver running, census or no census, was the sound of someone tampering with his cargo; and noise, all along, had been one of the biggest problems.

Opened Pete Duveen's ramp. Also the one on Allie's trailer.

While I did that, Bert brought several huge rolls of three-inch-thick latex from Owen's van and unrolled them down all the ramps, and across the bare patches of car park in between the boxes. I fetched the head-collar bought for the purpose from my bag and stepped into Jody's box. The black horse looked at me incuriously, standing there quietly in his traveling rug and four leg-guards. I checked his ear for the tiny nick and his shoulder for the bald pennyworth, and wasted a moment in patting him.

I knew all too well that success depended on my being able to persuade this strange four-footed creature to go with me gently and without fuss, and wished passionately for more expertise. All I had were nimble hands and sympathy, and they would have to be enough.

I unbuckled his rug at high speed and thanked the gods that the leg-guards Jody habitually used for traveling his horses were not laboriously wound-on bandages but lengths of plastic-backed foam rubber fastened by strips of Velcro.

I had all four off before Bert had finished the sound-proofing. Put the new head-collar over his neck; unbuckled and removed his own and left it swinging, still tied to the stall. Fitted and fastened the new one, and gave the rope a tentative tug. Energise took one step, then another, then with more assurance followed me sweetly down the ramp. If felt miraculous, but nothing like fast enough.

Hurry. Get the other horses, and hurry.

They didn't seem to mind walking on the soft spongy surface, but they wouldn't go fast. I tried to take them calmly, to keep my urgency to myself, to stop them taking fright and skittering away and crashing those metal-capped feet onto the car park.

Hurry. Hurry.

I had to get Energise's substitute into his place, wearing the right rug, the right bandages, and the right head-collar, before the box driver and the lad came out of the caravan.

Also his hoofs . . . Racing plates were sometimes put on by the blacksmith at home, who then rubbed on oil to obliterate the rasp marks of the file and give the feet a well-groomed appearance. I had brought hoof oil in my bag in case Energise had already had his shoes changed, and he had.

"Hurry, for gawd's sake," said Bert, seeing me fetch the oil. He was running back to the van with relays of rerolled latex and grinning like a Pools winner.

I painted the hoofs a glossy dark. Buckled on the swinging head-collar without disturbing the tethering knot, as the lad would notice if it was tied differently. Buckled the rug round the chest and under the belly. Fastened the Velcro strips on all four legguards. Shut the folding gates to his stall exactly as they had been before, and briefly looked back before closing the ramp. The black head was turned toward me, the liquid eye patient and unmoved. I smiled at him involuntarily, jumped out of the box, and with Bert's help eased shut the clips on the ramp.

Owen came out of the caravan, ran across, and fastened the ramp on the trailer. I jumped in with the horse in Pete's box. Bert lifted the ramp and did another silent job on the clips.

Through the windshield of Pete's box, the car park looked quiet and tidy.

Owen returned to the driving seat of his van and Bert walked back toward the road.

At the same instant, Jody's driver and lad hurried out of the caravan and tramped across to their horse box. I ducked out of sight, but I could hear one of them say, as he re-embarked, "Right lot of time-wasting cobblers, that was."

Then the engine throbbed to life, the box moved off, and Bert considerately held up a car or two so that it should have a clear passage back to its interrupted journey. If I hadn't had so much still to do, I would have laughed.

I fastened the rug. Tied the head-collar rope. Clipped on the leg-guards. I'd never worked so fast in my life.

What else? I glanced over my beautiful black horse, seeking things undone. He looked steadfastly back. I smiled at him, too, and told him he was a great fellow. Then Pete came out of the caravan and I scrambled through to the cab, and tried to sit in the passenger seat as if bored with waiting instead of sweating with effort and with a heart racing like tappets.

Pete climbed into his side of the cab and threw his logbook and license disgustedly onto the glove shelf. shelf.

"They're always stopping us nowadays. Spot check on logbooks. Spot check on vehicles. Half an hour a time, those. And now a census."

"Irritating," I agreed, making my voice a lot slower than my pulse.

His usual good nature returned in a smile. "Actually, the checks are a good thing. Some lorries, in the old days, were death on wheels. And some drivers, I dare say." He stretched his hand toward the ignition. "Where to?" he said.

"Might as well go back. As you say, the horse is quiet. If you could take me back to my car?"

"Sure thing," he said. "You're the boss."

Bert shepherded us solicitously onto the southbound lane, holding up the traffic with a straight face and obvious enjoyment. Pete drove steadily back to the lay-by and pulled in behind the Cortina.

"I expect you think it a wasted day," I said. "But I assure you from my point of view it's been worth it."

"That's all that matters," he said cheerfully.

"Take good care of this fellow going home," I

said, looking back at the horse. "And would you remind the lads in Mr. Ramsey's yard that I've arranged for a security guard to patrol the stable at night for a while? He should be arriving there later this afternoon."

"Sure," he said, nodding.

"That's all, then, I guess." I took my bag and jumped down from the cab. He gave me a final wave through the window, and set off again southward along the A-34.

I leaned against the Cortina, watching him go down the hill, across the valley, and up over the horizon on the far side.

I wondered how Energise would like his new home.

13

Charlie, Allie, Bert, and Owen were all in the caravan when I drove back there, drinking coffee and
laughing like kids.

"Here," Bert said, wheezing with joy. "A bleeding
police car came along a second after I'd picked up the
census notices and all those cones. Just a bleeding second."

"It didn't stop, I hope."

"Not a chance. Mind you, I'd taken off the fancy
clobber. First thing. The fuzz don't love you for imper-
sonating them, even if your hatband is only a bit of
bleeding ribbon painted in checks."

Charlie said, more soberly, "It was the only police
car we've seen."

"The cones were only in the road for about ten
minutes," Allie said. "It sure would have been
unlucky if the police had driven by in that time."

She was sitting by one of the desks looking neat
but unremarkable in a plain skirt and jersey. On the
desk stood my typewriter, uncovered, with piles of sta-
tionery alongside. Charlie, at the other desk, wore an
elderly suit, faintly shabby and a size too small. He
had parted his hair in the center and brushed it flat with
water, and had somehow contrived a look of mid-
dling bureaucracy instead of world finance. Before
him, too, lay an impressive array of official forms

and other literature, and the walls of the caravan were drawing-pinned with exhortative Ministry posters.

"How did you get all this bleeding junk?" said Bert, waving his hand at it.

"Applied for it," I said. "It's not difficult to get government forms or information posters. All you do is ask."

"Blimey."

"They're not census forms, of course. Most of them are application forms for driving licenses and passports, and things like that. Owen and I just made up the census questions and typed them out for Charlie, and he pretended to put the answers on the forms."

Owen drank his coffee with a happy smile, and Charlie said, chuckling, "You should have seen your man here putting on his obstructive act. Standing there in front of me like an idiot and either answering the questions wrong or arguing about answering them at all. The two men from the horse box thought him quite funny and made practically no fuss about being kept waiting. It was the other man, Pete Duveen, who was getting tired of it, but as he was at the back of the queue he couldn't do much."

"Four minutes," Owen said. "You said you needed a minimum of four. So we did our best."

"You must have given me nearer five," I said gratefully. "Did you hear anything?"

Allie laughed. "There was so much darned racket going on in here. Owen arguing, me banging away on the typewriter, the traffic outside, pop radio inside, and that heater. . . . How did you fix that heater?"

We all looked at the Calor gas heater that warmed the caravan. It clattered continually like a broken fan.

"Screwed a small swinging flap up at the top here, inside. The rising hot air makes it bang against the casing."

"Switch it off," Charlie said. "It's driving me mad."

I produced instead a screwdriver and undid the

necessary screws. Peace returned to the gas, and Charlie said he could see the value of a college education.

"Pete Duveen knew the other box driver," Allie said conversationally. "Seems they're all one big club."

"See each other every bleeding day at the races," Bert confirmed. "Here, that box driver made a bit of a fuss when I said the lad had to go into the caravan, too. Like you said, they aren't supposed to leave a race horse unguarded. So I said I'd bleeding guard it for him. How's that for a laugh? He said he supposed it was okay, as I was the police. I said I'd got instructions that everyone had to go into the census, no exceptions."

"People will do anything if it looks official enough," Charlie said, happily nodding.

"Well . . ." I put down my much needed cup of coffee and stretched my spine. "Time to be off, don't you think?"

"Right," Charlie said. "All this paper and stuff goes in Owen's van."

They began moving slowly, the reminiscent smiles still in place, packing the phony census into carrier bags. Allie came out with me when I left.

"We've had more fun," she said. "You can't imagine."

I supposed that I felt the same way, now that the flurry was over. I gave her a hug and a kiss and told her to take care of herself, and she said you, too.

"I'll call you this evening," I promised.

"I wish I was coming with you."

"We can't leave that here all day," I said, pointing to the Land-Rover and the trailer.

She smiled. "I guess not. Charlie says we'd all best be gone before anyone starts asking what we're doing."

"Charlie is a hundred percent right."

I went to Stratford-on-Avon races.

Drove fast, thinking of the righting of wrongs without benefit of lawyers. Thinking of the ephemeral quality of race horses and the snail's pace of litigation. Thinking that the best years of a hurdler's life could be wasted in stagnation while the courts deliberated to whom he belonged. Wondering what Jody would do when he found out about the morning's work, and hoping that I knew him well enough to have guessed right.

When I drew up in the racecourse car park just before the first race, I saw Jody's box standing among a row of others over by the entrance to the stables. The ramp was down, and from the general stage of activity I gathered that the horse was still on board.

I sat in my car a hundred yards away, watching through race glasses. I wondered when the lad would realize he had the wrong horse. I wondered if he would realize at all, because he certainly wouldn't expect to set off with one and arrive with another, and he would quite likely shrug off the first stirring of doubt. He was new in the yard since I had left, and with average luck, knowing Jody's rate of turnover, he would be neither experienced nor very bright.

Nothing appeared to be troubling him at that moment. He walked down the ramp carrying a bucket and a bundle of other equipment, and went through the gate to the stables. He looked about twenty. Long curly hair. Slight in build. Wearing flashy red trousers. I hoped he was thinking more of his own appearance than his horse's. I put the glasses down and waited.

My eye was caught by a woman in a white coat striding across the car park toward the horse boxes, and it took about five seconds before I realized with a jolt who she was.

Felicity Leeds.

Jody might have taken his knowing eyes to Chepstow, but Felicity had brought hers right here.

I hopped out of the car as if stung and made speed in her direction.

The lad came out of the stable, went up the ramp, and shortly reappeared, holding the horse's head. Felicity walked toward him as he began to persuade the horse to disembark.

"Felicity," I called.

She turned, saw me, looked appalled, threw a quick glance over her shoulder at the descending horse, and walked decisively toward me.

When she stopped, I looked over her shoulder and said with the sort of puzzlement that takes little to tip into suspicion. "What horse is that?"

She took another hurried look at the black hindquarters now disappearing toward the stable, and visibly gathered her wits.

"Padellic. Novice hurdler. Not much good."

"He reminds me . . ." I said slowly.

"First time out, today," Felicity said hastily. "Nothing much expected."

"Oh," I said, not sounding entirely reassured. "Are you going into the stables to see him, because I—"

"No," she said positively. "No need. He's perfectly all right." She gave me a sharp nod and walked briskly away to the main entrance to the course.

Without an accompanying trainer, no one could go into the racecourse stables. She knew I would have to contain my curiosity until the horse came out for its race, and until then, from her point of view, she was safe.

I, however, didn't want her visiting the stables herself. There was no particular reason why she should, as trainers mostly didn't when the journey from home to course was so short. All the same, I thought, I might as well fill up so much of her afternoon that she scarcely had time.

I came up with her again outside the weighing room, where she vibrated with tension from her patterned silk head-scarf to her high-heeled boots. There were sharp patches of color on her usually pale cheeks and her eyes regarding me with angry apprehension were as hot as fever.

"Felicity," I said. "Do you know anything about a load of muck that was dumped in my front garden?"

"A what?" The blank look she gave me was not quite blank enough.

I described at some length the component parts and

allover consistency of the obstruction, and remarked on their similarity to the discard pile at her own home.

"All muck heaps are alike," she said. "You couldn't tell where one particular load came from."

"All you'd need is a sample for forensic analysis."

"Did you take one?" she said sharply.

"No," I admitted.

"Well, then."

"You and Jody seem the most likely to have done it."

She looked at me with active dislike. "Everyone on the racecourse knows what a shit you've been to us. It doesn't surprise me at all that someone has expressed the same opinion in a concrete way."

"It surprises me very much that anyone except you should bother."

"I don't intend to talk about it," she said flatly.

"Well, I do," I said, and did, at some length, repetitively.

The muck heap accounted for a good deal of the afternoon, and Quintus, in a way, for the rest.

Quintus brought his noble brow and empty mind onto the stands and gave Felicity a peck on the cheek, lifting his hat punctiliously. To me, he donated what could only be called a scowl.

Felicity fell upon him as if he were a savior.

"I didn't know you were coming!" She sounded gladder than glad that he had.

"Just thought I would, you know, my dear."

She drew him away from me out of earshot and began talking to him earnestly. He nodded, smiling, agreeing with her. She talked some more. He nodded benignly, and patted her shoulder.

I moved towards her, for a final word on the matter.

"Oh, for God's sake, leave the bloody subject alone," Felicity exploded.

"What's the fella talking about?" Quintus said.

"A muck heap on his doorstep."

"Oh," Quintus said. "Ah . . ."

I described it all over again. I was getting quite attached to it, in retrospect.

Quintus was distinctly pleased. Chuckles quivered in his throat and his eyes twinkled with malice.

"Serves you right, what?" he said.

"Do you think so?"

"Shit to a shit," he said, nodding with satisfaction.

"*What* did you say?"

"Er . . . nothing."

Realization dawned on me with a sense of fitness. "You did it yourself," I said with conviction.

"Don't be ridiculous." He was still vastly amused.

"Lavatory humor would be *just* your mark."

"You are insulting." Less amusement, more arrogance.

"And the police took away the card you left to test it for fingerprints."

His mouth opened and shut. He looked blank. "The police?"

"Fellows in blue," I said.

Felity said furiously, "Trust someone like you not to take a joke."

"I'll take an apology," I said mildly. "In writing."

Their grudging admissions, their objections to an apology and the eventual drafting of that apology took care of a lot of time. It seems Quintus had hired a tip-up truck for his delivery and had required his gardener to do the actual work, while Jody and Felicity had generously contributed the load. Quintus had supervised its disposal and written his message.

He also, in his own hand and with bravado flourishes, wrote the apology. I thanked him courteously and told him I would frame it, which didn't please him in the least.

By that time, the fifth race was over and it was time to saddle the horses for the sixth.

Felicity, as the trainer's wife, was the natural person to supervise the saddling of their runner, and I knew that if she did she would realize she had the wrong horse.

On the other hand, I knew that if she did the saddling she couldn't stop me, as a member of the public, from taking a very close look, and from her point of view that was a risk she didn't want to take.

She solved her dilemma by getting Quintus to see to the saddling. Then, with a superhuman effort, she laid her hand on my arm in a conciliatory gesture and said, "All right. Let bygones be bygones. Let's go and have a drink."

"Sure," I said, expressing just the right amount of surprise and agreement. "Of course, if you'd like."

So we went off to the bar, where I bought her a large gin and tonic and myself a Scotch and water, and we stood talking about nothing much while we were both busy with private thoughts. She was trembling slightly from the force of hers, and I, too, had trouble preventing mine from showing. There we were, each trying his darnedest to keep the other away from the horse, she because she thought it was Energise and I because I knew it wasn't.

Felicity dawdled so long over her second drink that the horses were already leaving the parade ring and going out to the course when we finally made our way back to the heart of things. Quintus had understudied splendidly, and was to be seen giving a parting slap to the horse's rump. Felicity let her breath out in a sigh and dropped most of the pretense of being nice to me. When she left me abruptly to rejoin Quintus for the race, I made no move to stop her.

The horse put up a good show, considering.

There were twenty-two runners, none of them more than moderate, and they delivered the sort of performance that Energise would have left in the next parish. His substitute was running in his own class and finished undisgraced in sixth place, better than I would have expected. The crowd briefly cheered the winning favorite, and I thought it time to melt prudently and inconspicuously away.

I had gone to Stratford with more hope than certainty that the horse would actually run without the exchange being noticed. I had been prepared to do anything I reasonably could to achieve it, in order to give Ganser Mays the nasty shock of losing every penny he'd laid out on his squeezer.

What I hadn't actually bargained for was the effect the lost race would have on Felicity.

I saw her afterward, though I hadn't meant to, when she went to meet her returning horse. The jockey, a well-known rider who had doubtless been told to win, was looking strained enough, but Felicity seemed on the point of collapse.

Her face was a frightening white, her whole body shook, and her eyes looked as blank as marbles.

If I had ever wanted any personal revenge, I had it then, but I drove soberly away from the racecourse feeling sorry for her.

14

Rupert Ramsey met me with a stony face, not at all the expression one would normally expect from a successful trainer who had invited one of his owners to dinner.

"I'm glad you're early," he said forbiddingly. "Please come into the office."

I followed him across the hall into the familiar room, which was warm with a burning log fire. He made no move to offer me a drink, and I thought I might as well save him some trouble.

"You're going to tell me," I said, "that the horse which left here this morning is not the one which returned."

He raised his eyebrows. "So you don't deny it?"

"Of course not." I smiled. "I wouldn't have thought all that much of you if you hadn't noticed."

"The lad noticed. Donny. He told the head lad, and the head lad told me, and I went to see for myself. And what I want is an explanation."

"And it had better be good," I added, imitating his schoolmastery tone. He showed no amusement.

"This is no joke."

"Maybe not. But it's no crime, either. If you'll calm down a fraction, I'll explain."

"You have brought me a ringer. No trainer of any sense is going to stand for that." His anger was cold and deep.

I said, "The horse you thought was Energise was the ringer. And I didn't send him here. Jody did. The horse you have been trying to train for the Champion Hurdle, and which left here this morning, is a fairly useless novice called Padellic."

"I don't believe it."

"As Energise," I pointed out, "you have found him unbelievably disappointing."

"Well . . ." The first shade of doubt crept into his voice.

"When I discovered the wrong horse had been sent here, I asked you expressly not to run him in any races, because I certainly did not want you to be involved in running a ringer—nor myself, for that matter."

"But if you knew . . . why on earth didn't you immediately tell Jody he had made a mistake?"

"He didn't," I said simply. "He sent the wrong one on purpose."

He walked twice around the room in silence and then, still without a word, poured us each a drink.

"Right," he said, handing me a glass. "Pray continue."

I continued for quite a long while. He gestured to me to sit down, and sat opposite me and listened attentively.

"And this security firm," he said at the end. "Are you expecting Jody to try to get Energise back?"

I nodded. "He's an extremely determined man. I made the mistake once of underestimating his vigor and his speed, and that's what lost me Energise in the first place. I think when he got home from Chepstow and heard what Felicity and the box driver and the lad had to say, he would have been violently angry and would decide to act at once. He's not the sort to spend a day or so thinking about it. He'll come tonight. . . . I think and hope he will come tonight."

"He will be sure Energise is here?"

"He certainly should be," I said. "He'll ask his box driver about the journey and his box driver will tell him about the census. Jody will question closely and find that Pete Duveen was there, too. Jody will, I think, telephone to ask Pete Duveen if he saw anything unusual, and Pete, who has nothing to hide, will tell him he brought a black horse from here. He'll tell him he took a black horse home again. And he'll tell him I was there at the census point. I didn't ask him not to tell, and I am sure he will, because of his frank and open nature."

Rupert's lips twitched into the first hint of a smile. He straightened it out immediately. "I don't really approve of what you've done."

"Broken no laws," I said neutrally, neglecting to mention the shadowy area of Bert's police-impression uniform.

"Perhaps not." He thought it over. "And the security firm is here both to prevent the theft of Energise and to catch Jody red-handed?"

"Exactly so."

"I saw them in the yard this evening. Two uniformed men. They said they were expecting instructions from you when you arrived, though frankly at that point I was so angry with you that I was paying little attention."

"I talked to them on my way in," I said. "One will patrol the yard at regular intervals, and the other is going to sit outside the horse's box. I told them both to allow themselves to be enticed from their posts by any diversion."

"To *allow?*"

"Of course. You have to give the mouse a clear view of the cheese."

"Good God."

"And I wondered . . . whether you would consider staying handy, to act as a witness if Jody should come a-robbing."

It seemed to strike him for the first time that he, too, was Jody's victim. He began to look almost as Charlie had done, and certainly as Bert had done, as if he found countermeasures attractive. The tugging smile reappeared.

"It depends, of course, on what time Jody comes—if

he comes at all—but two of my guests tonight would be the best independent witnesses you could get. A lady magistrate and the local vicar."

"Will they stay late?" I asked.

"We can try." He thought for a bit. "What about the police?"

"How quickly can they get here if called?"

"Umm . . . Ten minutes. Quarter of an hour."

"That should be all right."

He nodded. A bell rang distantly in the house, signaling the arrival of more guests. He stood up, paused a moment, and frowned and said, "If the guard is to allow himself to be decoyed away, why plant him outside the horse's door in the first place?"

I smiled. "How else is Jody to know which box to rob?"

The dinner party seemed endless, though I couldn't afterward remember a word or a mouthful. There were eight at table, all better value than myself, and the vicar particularly shone because of his brilliance as a mimic. I half heard the string of imitated voices and saw everyone else falling about with hysterics, and could think only of my men outside in the winter night and of the marauder I hoped to entice.

To groans from his audience, the vicar played Cinderella at midnight and took himself off to shape up to Sunday, and three others shortly followed. Rupert pressed the last two to stay for nightcaps: the lady magistrate and her husband, a quiet young colonel with an active career and a bottomless capacity for port. He settled happily enough at the sight of a fresh decanter, and she with mock resignation continued a mild flirtation with Rupert.

The wheels inside my head whirred with the same doubts as in the morning. Suppose I had been wrong. Suppose Jody didn't come. Suppose he did come, but came unseen, and managed to steal the horse successfully.

Well . . . I'd planned for that, too. I checked for the

hundredth time through the "if"'s. I tried to imagine
what I hadn't already imagined, see what I hadn't seen,
prepare for the unprepared. Rupert cast an amused
glance or two at my abstracted expression and made no
attempt to break it down.

The doorbell rang sharply, three long insistent
pushes.

I stood up faster than good manners.

"Go on," Rupert said indulgently. "We'll be right
behind you, if you need us."

I nodded and departed, and crossed the hall to open
the front door. My man in a gray flannel suit stood
outside, looking worried and holding a torch.

"What is it?"

"I'm not sure. The other two are patrolling the yard
and I haven't seen them for some time. And I think we
have visitors, but they haven't come in a horse box."

"Did you see them? The visitors?"

"No. Only their car. Hidden off the road in a patch of
wild rhododendrons. At least . . . there is a car there
which wasn't there half an hour ago. What do you
think?"

"Better take a look," I said.

He nodded. I left the door of Rupert's house ajar, and
we walked together toward the main gate. Just inside it
stood the van that had brought the security guards, and
outside, less than fifty yards along the road, we came to
the car in the bushes, dimly seen even by torchlight.

"It isn't a car I recognize," I said. "Suppose it's just a
couple of lovers?"

"They'd be inside it on a night like this, not out
snogging in the freezing undergrowth."

"You're right."

"Let's take the rotor arm, to make sure."

We lifted the hood and carefully removed the essential piece of electrics. Then, shining the torch as little as
possible and going on grass whenever there was a
choice, we hurried back toward the stable. The night
was windy enough to swallow small sounds, dark

enough to lose contact at five paces, and cold enough to do structural damage to brass monkeys.

At the entrance to the yard, we stopped to look and listen.

No lights. The dark heavy bulk of buildings was more sensed than seen against the overcast sky.

No sounds except our own breath and the greater lungs of the wind. No sign of the two guards.

"What now?"

"We'll go and check the horse," I said.

We went into the main yard and skirted round its edges, which were paved with quieter concrete. The center was an expanse of crunchy gravel, a giveaway even for cats.

Box 14 had a chair outside it. A wooden kitchen chair planted prosaically with its back to the stable wall. No guard sat on it.

Quietly I slid back the bolts on the top half of the door and looked inside. There was a soft movement and the sound of a hoof rustling the straw. A second's flash of torch showed the superb black shape patiently standing half asleep in the dark, drowsing away the equine night.

I shut the door and made faint grating noises with the bolt.

"He's fine," I said. "Let's see if we can find the others."

He nodded. We finished the circuit of the main yard and started along the various branches, moving with caution and trying not to use the torch. I couldn't stop the eerie feeling growing that we were not the only couple groping about in the dark. I saw substance in shadows, and reached out fearfully to touch objects that were not there, but only darker patches in the pervading black. We spent five or ten minutes feeling our way, listening, taking a few steps, listening, going on. We completed the tour of the outlying rows of boxes, and saw and heard nothing.

"This is no good," I said quietly. "There isn't a sign of

them, and has it occurred to you that they are hiding from us, thinking we are the intruders?"

"Just beginning to wonder."

"Let's go back to the main yard."

We turned and retraced our steps, this time taking a short cut through a narrow alleyway between two sections of boxes. I was in front, so it was I who practically tripped over the huddled bundle on the ground.

I switched on the torch. Saw the neat navy uniform and the blood glistening red on the forehead. Saw the shut eyes and the lax limbs of the man who should have been sitting on the empty kitchen chair.

"Oh, God," I said desperately, and thought I would never ever forgive myself. I knelt beside him and fumbled for his pulse.

"He's alive," said my friend in the gray flannel suit. He sounded reassuring and confident. "Look at him breathing. He'll be all right, you'll see."

All I could see was a man who was injured because I'd stationed him in the path of danger. "I'll get a doctor," I said, standing up.

"What about the horse?"

"Damn the horse. This is more important."

"I'll stay here with him till you get back."

I nodded and set off anxiously toward the house, shining the torch now without reservations. If permanent harm came to that man because of me . . .

I ran.

Burst in through Rupert's front door and found him standing there in the hall talking to the lady magistrate and the colonel, who were apparently just about to leave. She was pulling a cape around her shoulders, and Rupert was holding the colonel's coat. They turned and stared at me like a frozen tableau.

"My guard's been attacked. Knocked out," I said. "Could you get him a doctor?"

"Sure," Rupert said calmly. "Who attacked him?"

"I didn't see."

"Job for the police?"

"Yes, please."

He turned to the telephone, dialing briskly. "What about the horse?"

"They didn't come in a horse box."

We both digested implications while he got the rescue services on the move. The colonel and the magistrate stood immobile in the hall with their mouths half open, and Rupert, putting down the telephone, gave them an authoritative glance.

"Come out into the yard with us, will you?" he said. "Just in case we need witnesses?"

They weren't trained to disappear rapidly at the thought. When Rupert hurried out the door with me at his heels, they followed more slowly after.

Everything still looked entirely quiet outside.

"He's in a sort of alley between two blocks of boxes," I said.

"I know where you mean," Rupert said, nodding. "But first we'll just check on Energise."

"Later."

"No. Now. Why bash the guard if they weren't after the horse?"

He made straight for the main yard, switched on all six external lights, and set off across the brightly illuminated gravel.

The effect was like a flourish of trumpets. Noise, light, and movement filled the space where silence and dark had been total.

Both halves of the door of box 14 swung open about a foot, and two dark figures catapulted through the gap.

"Catch them!" Rupert shouted.

There was only one way out of the yard, the broad entrance through which we had come. The two figures ran in curving paths toward the exit, one to one side of Rupert and me, one to the other.

Rupert rushed to intercept the smaller, who was suddenly, as he turned his head to the light, recognizable as Jody.

I ran for the larger. Stretched out. Touched him.

He swung a heavy arm and threw out a hip, and I literally bounced off him, stumbling and falling.

The muscles were rock hard. The sunglasses glittered.

The joker was ripping through the pack.

Jody and Rupert rolled on the gravel, one clutching, one punching, both swearing. I tried again at Muscles, with the same useless results. He seemed to hesitate over going to Jody's help, which was how I'd come to be able to reach him a second time, but finally decided on flight. By the time I was again staggering to my feet, he was on his way to the exit with the throttle wide open.

A large figure in navy blue hurtled straight at him from the opposite direction and brought him down with a diving hug round the knees. The sunglasses flew off in a shiny arc and the two large figures lay in a writhing mass, the blue uniform uppermost and holding his own. I went to his help and sat on Muscles's ankles, crushing his feet sidewise with no compunction at all. He screeched with pain and stopped struggling, but I fear I didn't immediately stand up.

Jody wrenched himself free from Rupert and ran past me. The colonel, who with his lady had been watching the proceedings with astonishment, decided it was time for some soldierly action and elegantly stuck out his foot.

Jody tripped and fell sprawling. The colonel put more energy into it, leaned down, and took hold of the collar of Jody's coat. Rupert, rallying, came to his aid, and between them they, too, more or less sat on Jody, pinning him to the ground.

"What now?" Rupert panted.

"Wait for the police," I said succinctly.

Muscles and Jody both heaved about a good deal at this plan but didn't succeed in freeing themselves. Muscles complained that I'd broken his ankle. Jody, under the colonel's professional ministrations, seemed to have difficulty saying anything at all. The colonel was in fact

so single-handedly efficient that Rupert stood up and
dusted himself down and looked at me speculatively.

I jerked my head in the direction of box 14, where
the door still stood half open, showing only darkness
within. He nodded slowly and went that way. Switched
on the light. Stepped inside. He came back with his
face grim and three bitter words.

"Energise is dead."

15

Rupert fetched some rope with which he ignominiously tied Jody's hands behind his back before he and the colonel let him get up, and the colonel held the free end of the rope so that Jody was to all intents on a lead. Once up, Jody aimed a kick at the colonel and Rupert told him to stop unless he wanted his ankles tied as well.

Rupert and my man in blue uniform did a repeat job on Muscles, whose ankles were not in kicking shape and whose language raised eyebrows even on the lady magistrate, who had heard more than most.

The reason for Muscles's ubiquitous sunglasses was at once apparent, now that one could see his face. He stood glowering like a bull, seething with impotent rage, hopping on one foot and pulling against the tethering rope that led back from his wrists to my man in blue. His eyelids, especially the lower, were grossly distorted, and even in the outside lighting looked bright pink with inflammation. One could pity his plight, which was clearly horrid.

"I know you," Rupert said suddenly, looking at him closely. "What's the matter with your eyes?"

"Mind your own effing business."

"Macrahinish. That's what your name is. Macrahinish."

Muscles didn't comment. Rupert turned to me.

"Don't you know him? Perhaps he was before your time. He's a vet. A struck-off vet. Struck off the vets' register and warned off the racecourse. And absolutely not allowed to set foot in a racing stable."

Muscles-Macrahinish delivered himself of an unflattering opinion of racing in general and Rupert in particular.

Rupert said, "He was convicted of doping and fraud and served a term in jail. He ran a big doping ring and supplied all the drugs. He looks older and there's something wrong with his eyes, but that's who this is, all right. Macrahinish."

I turned away from the group and walked over to the brightly lit loose-box. Swung the door wide. Looked inside.

My beautiful black horse lay flat on his side, legs straight, head limp on the straw. The liquid eye was dull and opaque, mocking the sheen that was still on his coat, and he still had pieces of unchewed hay half in and half out of his mouth. There was no blood, and no visible wound. I went in and squatted beside him, and patted him sadly with anger and regret.

Jody and Macrahinish had been unwillingly propelled in my wake. I looked up to find them inside the box, with Rupert, the colonel, his wife, and the man in blue effectively blocking the doorway behind them.

"How did you kill him?" I asked, the bitterness apparent in my voice.

Macrahinish's reply did not contain the relevant information.

I straightened up, and in doing so caught sight of a flat brown attaché case half hidden in the straw by the horse's tail. I bent down again and picked it up. The sight of it brought a sound and a squirm from Macrahinish, and he began to swear in earnest when I balanced it on the manger and unfastened the clips.

The case contained regular veterinarian equipment, neatly stowed in compartments. I touched only one thing, carefully lifting it out.

A plastic bag containing a clear liquid. A bag plainly proclaiming the contents to be sterile saline solution.

I held it out toward Jody and said, "You dripped alcohol straight into my veins."

"You were unconscious," he said disbelievingly.

"Shut up, you stupid fool," Macrahinish screamed at him.

I smiled. "Not all the time. I remember nearly everything about that night."

"He said he didn't," Jody said defensively to Macrahinish, and was rewarded by a look from the swollen eyes that would have made a nonstarter of Medusa.

"I went to see if you still had Energise," I said. "And I found you had."

"You don't know one horse from another," he sneered. "You're just a mug. A blind greedy mug."

"So are you," I said. "The horse you've killed is not Energise."

"It is!"

"Shut up!" screamed Macrahinish in fury. "Keep your stupid sodding mouth shut."

"No," I said to Jody. "The horse you've killed is an American horse called Black Fire."

Jody looked wildly down at the quiet body.

"It damn well is Energise," he insisted. "I'd know him anywhere."

"Jesus," Macrahinish shouted. "I'll cut your tongue out!"

Rupert said doubtfully to me, "Are you sure it's not Energise?"

"Positive."

"He's just saying it to spite me," said Jody furiously. "I know it's Energise. See that tiny bald patch on his shoulder? That's Energise."

Macrahinish, beyond speech, tried to attack him, tied hands and dicky ankle notwithstanding. Jody merely gave him a vague look, concentrating only on the horse.

"You are saying," Rupert suggested, "that you came to kill Energise, and that you've done it."

"Yes," said Jody triumphantly.

The word hung in the air, vibrating. No one said anything. Jody looked round at each watching face, at first with defiant angry pride, then with the first creeping of doubt, and finally with the realization of what Macrahinish had been trying to tell him: that he should never have been drawn into admitting anything. The fire visibly died into glum and chilly embers.

"I didn't kill him," he said sullenly. "Macrahinish did. I didn't want to kill him at all, but Macrahinish insisted."

A police car arrived with two young and persistent constables who seemed to find nothing particularly odd in being called to the murder of a horse.

They wrote in their notebooks that five witnesses, including a magistrate, had heard Jody Leeds admit that he and a disbarred veterinary surgeon had broken into a racing stable after midnight with the intention of putting to death one of the horses. They noted that a horse was dead. Cause of death, unknown until an autopsy could be arranged.

Hard on their heels came Rupert's doctor, an elderly man with a paternal manner. Yawning but uncomplaining, he accompanied me to find my security guard, who to my great relief was sitting on the ground with his head in his hands, awake and groaning healthily. We took him into Rupert's office, where the doctor stuck a plaster on the dried wound on his forehead, gave him some tablets, and told him to lay off work for a couple of days. He smiled weakly and said it depended if his boss would let him.

One of the young policemen asked if he'd seen who had hit him.

"Big man with sunglasses. He was creeping along behind me, holding a ruddy great chunk of wood. I heard something. . . . I turned and shone my torch, and there he was. He swung at my head. Gave me a right crack, he did. Next thing I knew, I was lying on the ground."

Reassured by his revival, I went outside again to see what was happening.

The magistrate and the colonel seemed to have gone home, and Rupert was down in the yard talking to some of his stable staff who had been wakened by the noise.

Macrahinish was hopping about on one leg, accusing me of having broken the other, and swearing he'd have me prosecuted for using undue force to protect my property. The elderly doctor phlegmatically examined the limb in question and said that in his opinion it was a sprain.

The police had rashly untied the Macrahinish wrists and were obviously relying on the leg injury to prevent escape. At the milder word "sprain," they produced handcuffs and invited Macrahinish to stick his arms out. He refused and resisted, and because they, as I had done, underestimated both his strength and his violence, it took a hectic few minutes for them to make him secure.

"Resisting arrest," they panted, writing it in the note-books. "Attacking police officers in the course of their duty."

Macrahinish's sunglasses lay on the gravel in the main yard, where he had lost them in the first tackle. I walked down to where they shone in the light and picked them up. Then I took them slowly back to him and put them in his handcuffed hands.

He stared at me through the raw-looking eyelids. He said nothing. He put the sunglasses on, and his fingers were trembling.

"Ectropion," said the doctor as I walked away.

"What?" I said.

"The condition of his eyes. Ectropion. Poor fellow."

The police made no mistakes with Jody. He sat stiffly beside Macrahinish in the back of the police car with handcuffs on his wrists. When the police went to close the doors, ready to leave, he leaned forward and spoke to me through rigid lips.

"You *shit*," he said.

Rupert invited the rest of my security firm indoors for warmth and coffee, and in his office I introduced them to him.

"My friend in gray flannel," I said, "is Charlie Canterfield. My big man in blue is Bert Huggerneck. My injured friend with the dried blood on his face is Owen Idris."

Rupert shook hands with each, and they grinned at him. He sensed immediately that there was more in their smiles than he would have expected, and he turned his inquiring gaze on me.

"Which firm do they come from?" he asked.

"Charlie's a merchant banker, Bert's a bookies' clerk, and Owen helps in my workshop."

Charlie chuckled, and said in his fruitiest Eton, "We also run a nice line in a census, if you should ever need one."

Rupert shook his head helplessly and fetched brandy and glasses from a cupboard.

"If I ask questions," he said, pouring lavishly, "will you answer them?"

"If we can," I said.

"That dead horse in the stable. Is it Energise?"

"No. As I said, it's a horse I bought in the States, called Black Fire."

"But the bald patch . . . Jody was so certain."

"I did that bald patch with a razor blade. The horses were extraordinarily alike, apart from that. Especially at night, because of being black. But there's one certain way of identifying Black Fire. He has his American racing number tattooed inside his lip."

"Why did you bring him here?"

"I didn't want to risk the real Energise. Before I saw Black Fire in America, I couldn't see how to entice Jody safely. Afterwards, it was easier."

"But I didn't get the impression earlier this evening," Rupert said pensively, "that you expected them to kill the horse."

"No . . . I didn't know about Macrahinish. I mean, I didn't know he was a vet, or that he could overrule Jody. I expected Jody just to try to steal the horse, and I wanted to catch him in the act. Catch him physically committing a positive criminal act which he couldn't possibly explain away. I wanted to force the racing authorities, more than the police, to see that Jody was not the innocent little underdog they believed."

Rupert thought it over. "Why didn't you think he would kill him?"

"Well . . . it did cross my mind, but on balance I thought it unlikely, because Energise is such a good horse. I thought Jody would want to hide him away somewhere, so that he could make a profit on him later, even if he sold him as a point-to-pointer. Energise represents money, and Jody has never missed a trick in that direction."

"But Macrahinish wanted him dead," Rupert said.

I sighed. "I suppose he thought it safer."

Rupert smiled. "You had put them in a terrible fix. They couldn't risk you being satisfied with getting your horse back. They couldn't be sure you couldn't somehow prove they had stolen it originally. But if you no longer had it, you would have found it almost impossible to make allegations stick."

"That's right," Charlie agreed. "That's exactly what Steven thought."

"Also," I said, "Jody wouldn't have been able to bear the thought of me getting the better of him. Apart from safety and profit, he would have taken Energise back simply for revenge."

"You know what?" Charlie said. "It's my guess that he probably put his entire bank balance on Padellic at Stratford, thinking it was Energise, and when Padellic turned up sixth he lost the lot. And that in itself is a tidy little motive for revenge."

"Here," Bert said appreciatively. "I wonder how much Ganser bleeding Mays is down the drain for!

Makes you bleeding laugh, don't it? There they all were, thinking they were backing a ringer, and we'd gone and put the real Padellic back where he belonged."

"Trained by Rupert," I murmured, "to do his best."

Rupert looked at us one by one and shook his head. "You're a lot of rogues."

We drank our brandy and didn't dispute it.

"Where did the American horse come from?" Rupert asked.

"Miami."

"No . . . This morning."

"A quiet little stable in the country," I said. "We had him brought to the census point—"

"And you should have bleeding seen him," Bert interrupted gleefully. "Our ca*pit*alist here, I mean. Whizzing these three horses in and out of horse boxes faster than the three-card trick."

"I must say," Rupert said thoughtfully, "that I've wondered just how he managed it."

"He took bleeding Energise out of Jody's box and put it in the empty stall of the trailer which brought Black Fire. Then he put Padellic where Energise had been, in Jody's box. Then he put Black Fire where Padellic had been—in your box, that is. All three of them buzzing in a circle like a bleeding merry-go-round."

Charlie said, smiling, "All change at the census. Padellic started from here and went to Stratford. Black Fire started from the country and came here. And Energise started from Jody's—" He stopped.

"And went to where?" Rupert asked.

I shook my head. "He's safe, I promise you." Safe with Allie at Hantsford Manor, with Miss Johnston and Mrs. Fairchild-Smith. "We'll leave him where he is for a week or two."

"Yeah," Bert said, explaining. "Because, see, we've had Jody Leeds and that red-eyed hunk of muscle of his exploding all over us with temper-temper, but what about that other one? What about that other one we've kicked right where it hurts, eh? We don't want to risk Energise getting the chop after all from Mr. Squeezer bleeding Ganser down the bleeding drain Mays."

16

Owen and I went back to London. I drove, with him sitting beside me fitfully dozing and pretending in betweentimes that he didn't have a headache.

"Don't be silly," I said. "I know what it feels like. You've got a proper thumper, and notwithstanding that snide crack to the doctor about your boss not letting you take a couple of days off, that's what you're going to get."

He smiled.

"I'm sorry about your head," I said.

"I know."

"How?"

"Charlie said."

I glanced across at him. His face in the glow from the dashboard looked peaceful and contented. "It's been," he said drowsily, "a humdinger of a day."

It was four in the morning when we reached the house and pulled into the driveway. He woke up slowly and shivered, his eyes fuzzy with fatigue.

"You're sleeping in my bed," I said, "and I'm taking the sofa." He opened his mouth. "Don't argue," I added.

"All right."

I locked the car and we walked to the front door, and that's where things went wrong.

The front door was not properly shut. Owen was too

208

sleepy to comprehend at once, but my heart dropped to pavement level the instant I saw it.

Burglars, I thought dumbly. Today of all days.

I pushed the door open. Everything was quiet. There was little furniture in the hall and nothing looked disturbed.

"What is it?" said Owen, realizing that something was wrong.

"The workshop door," I said, pointing.

"Oh, no."

That, too, was ajar, and there was no question of the intruder having used a key. The whole lock area was split, the raw wood showing in jagged layers up and down the jamb.

We walked along the carpeted passage, pushed the door wider, and took one step through onto concrete.

One step, and stopped dead.

The workshop was an area of complete devastation.

All the lights were on. All the cupboard doors and drawers were open, and everything that should have been in them was out and scattered and smashed. The workbenches were overturned and the racks of tools were torn from their moorings, and great chunks of plaster had been gouged out of the walls.

All my designs and drawings had been ripped to pieces. All the prototype toys seemed to have been stamped on.

Tins of oil and grease had been opened, and the contents emptied onto the mess, and the paint I'd used on the census notices was splashed on everything the oil had missed.

The machines themselves . . .

I swallowed. I was never going to make anything else on those machines. Not ever again.

Not burglars, I thought aridly.

Spite.

I felt too stunned to speak and I imagine it was the same with Owen, because for an appreciable time we both just stood there, immobile and silent. The mess

before us screamed out its message of viciousness and
evil, and the intensity of the hate that had committed
such havoc made me feel sick.

On feet that seemed disconnected from my legs, I
took a couple of steps forward.

There was a flicker of movement on the edge of my
vision away behind the half-open door. I spun on my
toe with every primitive instinct raising hairs in instant
alarm, and what I saw allowed no reassurance whatso-
ever.

Ganser Mays stood there, waiting like a hawk. The
long nose seemed a sharp beak, and his eyes behind
the metal-rimmed spectacles glittered with mania. He
was positioning his arms for a scything downward
swing, which was the movement I'd seen, and in his
hands he held a heavy long-handled axe.

I leaped sidewise a thousandth of a second before
the killing edge swept through the place where I'd been
standing.

"Get help!" I shouted breathlessly to Owen. "Get
out and get help!"

I had a blurred impression of Owen's strained face,
mouth open, eyes huge, dried blood still dark on his
cheek. For an instant he didn't move and I thought he
wouldn't go, but when next I caught a glimpse of the
doorway, it was empty.

Whether or not he'd been actually lying in wait for
me, there was no doubt that now I was there, Ganser
Mays was going to try to do to me what he'd already
done to my possessions. I learned a good deal from him
in the next few minutes. I learned about mental terror.
Learned about extreme physical fear. Learned that it
was no fun at all facing, unarmed and untrained, a
man with the will and the weapon for murder.

What was more, it was my own axe.

We played an obscene sort of hide-and-seek round
the wrecked machines. It only needed one of the fero-
cious chops to connect, and I would be without arm or
leg if not without life. He slashed whenever he could
get near enough, and I hadn't enough faith in my speed

or strength to try to tackle him within slicing range. I dodged always and precariously, circling the ruined lathe, the milling machine, the hacksaw, back to the lathe, putting the precious bulks of metal between me and death.

Up and down the room, again and again.

There was never a rigid line between sense and insanity, and maybe by some definitions Ganser Mays was sane. Certainly in all that obsessed destructive fury he was aware enough that I might escape through the door. From the moment I'd first stepped past him into the workshop, he gave me no chance to reach safety that way.

There were tools scattered on the floor from the torn-down racks, but they were mostly small and, in any case, not round the machines but on the opposite side of the workshop. I could leave the shelter of the row of machines and cross open space to try to arm myself . . . but nothing compared in weight or usefulness with that axe, and chisels and saws and drill bits weren't worth the danger of exposure.

If Owen came back with help, maybe I could last out.

Shortage of breath . . . I was averagely fit, but no athlete . . . couldn't pull in enough oxygen for failing muscles . . . felt fatal weaknesses slowing my movements . . . knew I couldn't afford to slip on the oil or stumble over the bolts mooring the baseplates to the floor or leave my hands holding on to anything for more than a second for fear of severed fingers.

He seemed tireless, both in body and intent. I kept my attention more on the axe than on his face, but the fractional views I caught of his fixed, fanatical, and curiously rigid expression gave no room for hope that he would stop before he had achieved his object. Trying to reason with him would have been like arguing with an avalanche. I didn't try.

Breath sawed through my throat. Owen . . . Why didn't he bloody well hurry? If he didn't hurry, he might as well come back tomorrow for all the good it would do me. . . .

The axe crashed down so close to my shoulder that I shuddered from imagination and began to despair. He was going to kill me. I was going to feel the bite of that heavy steel, to know the agony and see the blood spurt, to be chopped and smashed like everything else.

I was up at the end where the electric motor that worked all the machines was located. He was four feet away, swinging, looking merciless and savage. I was shaking, panting, and still trying frantically to escape, and it was more to distract him for a precious second than from any devious plan that I took the time to kick the main switch from off to on.

The engine hummed and activated and main belt, which turned the big wheel near the ceiling and rotated the long shaft down the workshop. All the belts to the machines began slapping as usual, except that this time half of them had been cut right through and the free ends flapped in the air like streamers.

That took his eye off me but for only a blink. As I circled the electric motor, which was much smaller than the machines and not good cover, he brought his head back toward me with a snap.

And he saw that I was exposed. A flash of triumph crossed his pale sweating face. He whipped the axe back and high and struck at me with all his strength.

I jumped sidewise in desperation, slipped and fell, and thought as I went down that this was it. . . . This was the end. . . . He would be on me before I could get up.

I half saw the axe go up again as I lunged out with one foot in a desperate kick at his ankles. Connected. Threw him a fraction off balance. Only a matter of a few inches: and it didn't affect the weight of his downward swing, but only its direction. Instead of burying itself in me, the blade sank into the main belt driving the machines, and for one fatal moment Ganser Mays hung on to the shaft. Whether he thought I had somehow grasped the axe and was trying to tug it away from him, heaven knows. In any case he gripped tight, and the whirling belt swept him off his feet.

The belt moved at about ten feet a second. It took one second for Ganser Mays to reach the big wheel above. I dare say he let go of the shaft at about that point, but the wheel caught him and crushed him in the small space between itself and the ceiling.

He screamed, a short loud cry of extremity, chokingly cut off.

The wheel inexorably whirled him through and out the other side. It would have taken more than a soft human body to stop a motor that drove machine tools.

He fell from the high point and thumped sickeningly onto the concrete not far from where I was still scrambling to get up. It had happened at such immense speed that he had been up to the ceiling and down again before I could find my feet.

The axe had been dislodged and had fallen separately beside him—near his hand, as if all he had to do was stretch out six inches and he would be back in business.

But Ganser Mays was never going to be back in business. I stood looking down at him while the engine hummed and the big killing wheel rotated as impersonally as usual, and the remaining belts to the machines slapped quietly as they always did.

There was little blood. His face was white. The spectacles had gone and the eyes were half open. The sharp nose was angled strangely sidewise. The neck was bent at an impossible angle; and whatever else had broken, that was enough.

I stood there for a while panting for breath and sweating, and trembling from fatigue and the screwed tension of past fear. Then whatever strength I had left drained abruptly away, and I sat on the floor beside the electric motor and drooped an arm over it for support like a wilted lily. Beyond thought. Beyond feeling. Just dumbly and excruciatingly exhausted.

It was at that moment that Owen returned. The help he'd brought wore an authentic navy-blue uniform and a real black-and-white checkered band on his cap. He took a long slow look and summoned reinforcements.

Hours later, when they had all gone, I went back downstairs to the workshop.

Upstairs nothing, miraculously, had been touched. Either our return had interrupted the program before it had got that far or the workshop had been the only intended target. In any case my first sight of the peaceful sitting room had been a flooding relief.

Owen and I had flopped weakly around in armchairs while the routine police work ebbed and flowed, and after lengthy question-and-answer sessions and the departure of the late Mr. Mays we finally had found ourselves alone.

It was already Sunday morning. The sun, with no sense of fitness, was brightly shining. Regent's Park sparkled with frost and the puddles were glazed with ice.

"Go to bed," I said to Owen.

He shook his head. "Think I'll go home."

"Come back when you're ready."

He smiled. "Tomorrow," he said. "For a spot of sweeping up."

When he'd gone, I wandered aimlessly about, collecting coffee cups and emptying ashtrays and thinking disconnected thoughts. I felt both too tired and too unsettled for sleep, and it was then that I found myself going back to the devastation in the workshop.

The spirit of the dead man had gone. The place no longer vibrated with violent hate. In the morning light it looked a cold and sordid shambles, squalid debris of a spent orgy.

I walked slowly down the room, stirring things with my toe. The work of twenty years lay there in little pieces. Designs torn like confetti. Toys crushed flat. Nothing could be mended or saved.

I supposed I could get duplicates at least of the design drawings if I tried, because copies were lodged in the patents' office. But the originals and all the handmade prototype toys were gone for good.

I came across the remains of the merry-go-round that I had made when I was fifteen. The first Rola: the beginning of everything. I squatted down and touched the pieces, remembering that distant decisive summer when I'd spent day after day in my uncle's workshop with ideas gushing like newly drilled oil out of a brain that was half child, half man.

I picked up one of the little horses. The blue one, with a white mane and tail. The one I'd made last of the six.

The golden barley-sugar rod that had connected it to the revolving roof was snapped off jaggedly an inch above the horse's back. One of the front legs was missing, and one of the ears.

I turned it over regretfully in my hands and looked disconsolately around at the mess. Poor little toys. Poor beautiful little toys, broken and gone.

It had cost me a good deal, one way and another, to get Energise back.

Turn the handle, Charlie had said, and all the little toys would revolve on their spindles and do what they should. But people weren't toys, and Jody and Macrahinish and Ganser Mays had jumped violently off their spindles and stripped the game out of control.

If I hadn't decided to take justice into my own hands, I wouldn't have been kicked or convicted of drunkenness. I would have saved myself the price of Black Fire and a host of other expenses. I wouldn't have put Owen at risk as a guard, and I wouldn't have felt responsible for the ruin of Jody and Felicity, the probable return to jail of Macrahinish, and the death of Ganser Mays.

Pointless to say that I hadn't meant them so much harm, or that their own violence had brought about their own doom. It *was* I who had given them the first push.

Should I have done it?

Did I wish I hadn't?

I straightened to my feet and smiled ruefully at the shambles, and knew that the answer to both questions was no.

Epilogue

I gave Energise away.

Six weeks after his safe return to Rupert's stable, he ran in the Champion Hurdle, and I took a party to Cheltenham to cheer him on. A sick tycoon having generously lent his private box, we went in comfort, with lunch before and champagne after and a lot of smiling in between.

The four newly registered joint owners were having a ball and slapping each other on the back with glee: Bert, Allie, Owen, and Charlie, as high in good spirits as they'd been at the census.

Charlie had brought the bridge-playing wife and Bert his fat old mum, and Owen had shyly and unexpectedly produced an unspoiled daughter of sixteen. The oddly mixed party proved a smash-hit success, my four conspirators carrying it along easily on the strength of liking each other a lot.

While they all went off to place bets and look at the horses in the parade ring, I stayed up in the box. I stayed there most of the afternoon. I had found it impossible, as the weeks passed, to regain my old innocent enthusiasm for racing and there was still a massive movement of support and sympathy for Jody, which I supposed would never change. Letters to sporting papers spoke of sympathy for his misfortunes and disgust for the one who had brought them about. Racing columnists, though reluctantly convinced of his villainy, referred to him still as the "unfortunate" Jody. Quintus, implacably resentful, was ferreting away against me in the Jockey Club and telling everyone it was my fault his son had made "misjudgments." I had asked him how it could possibly be my fault that Jody had made the misjudgment of taking Macrahinish and Ganser Mays for associates, and had received no answer.

Also I had heard, unofficially (because the interesting facts could not be generally broadcast on account of the forthcoming trial and my high-up police informant had made me promise not to repeat them), the results of the autopsy on Black Fire. He had been killed by a massive dose of chloroform injected between the ribs, straight into the heart. Quick, painless, and positively the work of a practiced hand.

The veterinary bag found beside the dead horse had contained a large hypodermic syringe with a sufficient length of needle; there were traces of chloroform inside the syringe and Macrahinish's fingerprints outside.

Jody and Macrahinish were out on bail, and the racing authorities had postponed their own inquiry until the law's verdict should be known. Jody still technically held his trainer's license.

The people who to my mind had shown most sense had been Jody's other owners. One by one they had melted apologetically away, reluctant to be had for mugs. They had judged without waiting around for a jury, and Jody had no horses left to train. And that in itself, in many eyes, was a further crying shame to be laid at my door.

I went out onto the balcony of the kind tycoon's box and stared vacantly over Cheltenham racecourse. Moral victory over Jody was impossible, because too many people still saw him, despite everything, as the poor hard-working little man who had fallen foul of the rich robber baron.

Charlie came out onto the balcony in my wake.

"Steven? What's the matter? You're too damned quiet."

"What we did," I said, sighing, "has changed nothing."

"Of course it has," he said robustly. "You'll see. Public opinion works awful slowly. People don't like doing about-turns and admitting they were fooled. But you trust your Uncle Charlie, this time next year, when they've got over their red faces, a lot of people will be quietly finding you're one of their best friends."

"Yeah," I said.

"Quintus," he said positively, "is doing himself a lot of personal no good just now with the hierarchy. The *on dit* round the bazaars is that if Quintus can't see his son is a full-blown criminal he is even thicker than anyone thought. I tell you, the opinion where it matters is one hundred percent for you, and our little private enterprise is the toast of the cigar circuit."

I smiled. "You make me feel better, even if you lie in your teeth."

"As God's my judge," he said virtuously, and spoiled it by glancing a shade apprehensively skyward.

"I saw Jody," I said. "Did you know?"

"No!"

"In the City," I said, nodding. "Him and Felicity, coming out of some law offices."

"What happened?"

"He spat," I said.

"How like him."

They had both looked pale and worried, and had stared at me in disbelief. Jody's ball of mucus had landed at my feet, punctuation mark of how he felt. If I'd known they were likely to be there, I would have avoided the district by ten miles, but since we were face-to-face I asked him straight out the question I most wanted answered.

"Did you send Ganser Mays to smash my place up?"

"He told him how to make you suffer," Felicity said spitefully. "Serves you right."

She cured in that one sentence the pangs of conscience I'd had about the final results of the Energise shuttle.

"You're a bloody fool, Jody," I said. "If you'd dealt straight with me, I'd've bought you horses to train for the Classics. With your ability, if you'd been honest, you could have gone to the top. Instead, you'll be warned off for life. It is you, believe me, who is the mug."

They had both stared at me sullenly, eyes full of frustrated rage. If either of them should have a chance in the future to do me further bad turns, I had no doubt that they would. There is no one as vindictive as the man who's done you wrong and been found out.

Charlie said, beside me, "Which do you think was the boss? Jody or Macrahinish or Ganser Mays?"

"I don't know," I said. "How does a triumvirate grab you?"

"Equal power?" He considered. "Might well be, I suppose. Just three birds of a feather drawn to each other by natural evil, stirring it in unholy alliance."

"Are all criminals so full of hate?"

"I dare say. I don't know all that many. Do you?"

"No."

"I should think," Charlie said, "that the hate comes first. Some people are just natural haters. Some bully the weak, some become anarchists, some rape women, some steal with maximum mess . . . and all of them enjoy the idea of the victim's pain."

"Then you can't cure a hater," I said.

"With hard-liners, not a chance."

Charlie and I contemplated this somber view and the others came back waving Tote tickets and bubbling over with good humor.

"Here," Bert said, slapping me on the back. "Know what I just heard? Down in the ring, see. All those bleeding little bookies that we saved from going bust over Padellic, they're passing round the bleeding hat."

"Just what, Bert," said Allie, "do you bleeding mean?"

"Here!" A huge grin spread across Bert's rugged features. "You're a right smashing bit of goods, you are, Allie, and that's a fact. What I mean is, those little guys are making a bleeding collection all round the country, and every shop the smart alecks tried it on with, they're all putting a fiver in, and they're going to send it to the Injured Jockey's bleeding Fund in honor of the firm of Scott, Canterfield, Ward, Idris & Huggerneck, what saved them all from disappearing down the bleeding plughole."

We opened a bottle of champagne on the strength of it, and Charlie said it was the eighth wonder of the world.

When the time came for the Champion Hurdle, we all went down to see Energise saddled. Rupert, busy fastening buckles, looked at the ranks of shining eyes and smiled with the indulgence of the longtime professional. The horse himself could scarcely stand still, so full was he of oats and health and general excitement. I patted his elegant black neck, and he tossed his head and sprayed me with a blow through his nostrils.

I said to Rupert, "Do you think I'm too old to learn to ride?"

"Race horses?" He pulled tight the second girth and fastened the buckle.

"Yes."

He slapped the black rump. "Come down Monday morning and make a start."

"In front of all the lads?"

"Well?" He was amused, but it was an exceptional offer. Few trainers would bother.

"I'll be there," I said.

Donny led Energise from the saddling boxes to the parade ring, closely followed by Rupert and the four new owners.

"But you're coming as well," Allie said, protesting.

I shook my head. "Four owners to one horse is enough."

Bert and Charlie tugged her with them, and they all stood in a little smiling group with happiness coming out of their ears. Bert's mum, Owen's daughter, and Charlie's wife went off to plunder the Tote, and I, with the most reputable bookmaking firm in the business, bet five hundred pounds to three thousand that Energise would win.

We watched him from the balcony of the private box with hearts thumping like jungle drums. It was for this that we had gone to so much trouble, this few minutes ahead. For the incredible pleasure of seeing a superb creature do what he was bred, trained, endowed, and eager for. For speed, for fun, for exhilaration, for love.

The tapes went up and they were away, the fourteen best hurdlers in Britain out to decide which was king.

Two miles of difficult undulating track. Nine flights of whippy hurdles. They crossed the first and the second and swept up the hill past the stands, with Energise lying sixth and moving easily, his jockey still wearing my distinctive bright-blue colors because none of his new owners had any.

"Go on, boyo," Owen said, his face rapt. "Slaughter the bloody lot of them." Generations of fervent Welshmen echoed in his voice.

Round the top of the course. Downhill to the dip. More jumps, then the long climb on the far side. One horse fell, bringing a gasp like a gale from the stands and a moan from Allie that she couldn't bear to watch. Energise flowed over the hurdles with the economy of all great jumpers and at the top of the far hill he lay fourth.

"Get your bleeding skates on," muttered Bert, whose knuckles showed white with clutching his race glasses. "Don't bleeding hang about."

Energise obeyed the instructions. Down the leg-testing slope he swooped like a black bird, racing level with the third horse, level with the second, pressing on the leader.

Over the next, three of them in line like a wave. Round the last bend swept all three in a row, with nothing to choose and all to be fought for over the last of the hurdles and the taxing, tiring, pull-up to the winning post.

"I can't bear it," Allie said. "Oh, come on, you great . . . gorgeous . . ."

"Slaughter them, boyo!"

"Shift, you bleeding . . ."

The voices shouted, the crowd yelled, and Charlie had tears in his eyes.

They came to the last flight all in a row, with Energise nearest the rails, furthest from the stands. He met it right, and jumped it cleanly, and I had stopped breathing.

The horse in the middle hit the top of the hurdle, twisted in the air, stumbled on landing, and fell in a skidding, sliding, sprawling heap. He fell toward Energise, who had to dodge sidewise to avoid him.

Such a little thing. A half-second's hesitation before he picked up his stride. But the third of the three, with a clear run, started away from the hurdle with a gain of two lengths.

Energise put his soul into winning that race. Stretched out and fought for every inch. Showed what gut and muscle could do on the green turf. Shortened the gap and closed it, and gained just a fraction at every stride.

Allie and Owen and Bert and Charlie were screaming like maniacs, and the winning post was too near, too near.

Energise finished second, by a short head.

It's no good expecting fairy-tale endings, in racing.

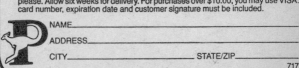